DISCOVER • CONNECT • TAKE ACTION
TROOP LEADER
planner

IF FOUND, PLEASE RETURN TO:

....

....

....

©2019 Wild Simplicity Paper Co.
All rights reserved.

SAMPLE PAGES

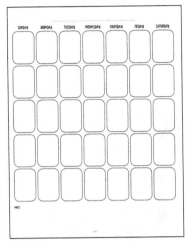

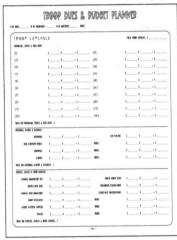
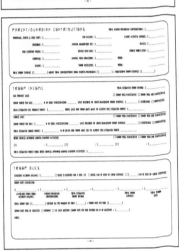

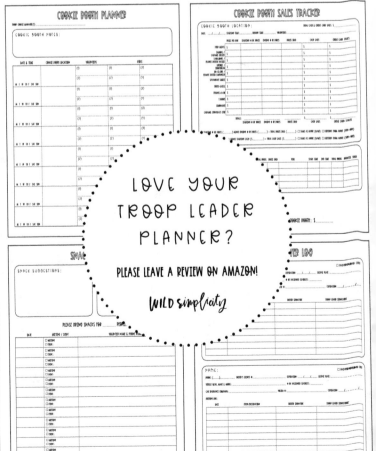

LOVE YOUR TROOP LEADER PLANNER?

PLEASE LEAVE A REVIEW ON AMAZON!

WILD simplicity

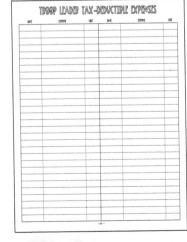
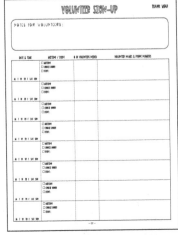

TABLE OF CONTENTS

TROOP INFORMATION

- TROOP LEADER & VOLUNTEER CONTACT INFORMATION 4
- SERVICE UNIT INFORMATION & CONTACTS 7
- COUNCIL INFORMATION & CONTACTS 8
- TROOP ROSTER 9
- TROOP BIRTHDAYS 19

CALENDARS

- YEAR-AT-A-GLANCE (UNDATED) 20
- MONTHLY CALENDARS (12 MONTHS, UNDATED) 22

PLANNERS & TRACKERS

- MEETING PLANNER 34
- BADGE ACTIVITIES PLANNER 70
- FLEXIBLE TRACKER FOR DUES, ATTENDANCE, BADGES, ETC. 90

FINANCES

- TROOP DUES & BUDGET PLANNER 100
- TROOP FINANCES 102
- TROOP LEADER TAX-DEDUCTIBLE EXPENSES 104
- TROOP LEADER TAX-DEDUCTIBLE MILEAGE 105

PRODUCT SALES

- COOKIE BOOTH PLANNER 106
- COOKIE BOOTH SALES TRACKER 108
- FLEXIBLE TRACKER FOR FALL PRODUCT SALES, COOKIES, ETC. 118

VOLUNTEER LOGS

- VOLUNTEER SIGN-UP SHEET 122
- SNACK SIGN-UP SHEET 128
- VOLUNTEER DRIVER LOG 130

MISCELLANEOUS

- TO-DO LISTS & NOTES 138

TROOP LEADER & VOLUNTEER CONTACT INFORMATION

TROOP LEADER ☐ BACKGROUND CHECK
NAME: .... EMAIL: ....
PHONE: (......) .... ADDRESS: ....
NOTES:

TROOP LEADER ☐ BACKGROUND CHECK
NAME: .... EMAIL: ....
PHONE: (......) .... ADDRESS: ....
NOTES:

ROLE: ☐ BACKGROUND CHECK
NAME: .... EMAIL: ....
PHONE: (......) .... ADDRESS: ....
NOTES:

ROLE: ☐ BACKGROUND CHECK
NAME: .... EMAIL: ....
PHONE: (......) .... ADDRESS: ....
NOTES:

ROLE: ☐ BACKGROUND CHECK
NAME: .... EMAIL: ....
PHONE: (......) .... ADDRESS: ....
NOTES:

"How wonderful it is that nobody need wait a single moment before starting to improve the world."
ANNE FRANK

ROLE: ☐ BACKGROUND CHECK
NAME: .... EMAIL: ....
PHONE: (......)................ ADDRESS: ....
NOTES:

ROLE: ☐ BACKGROUND CHECK
NAME: .... EMAIL: ....
PHONE: (......)................ ADDRESS: ....
NOTES:

ROLE: ☐ BACKGROUND CHECK
NAME: .... EMAIL: ....
PHONE: (......)................ ADDRESS: ....
NOTES:

ROLE: ☐ BACKGROUND CHECK
NAME: .... EMAIL: ....
PHONE: (......)................ ADDRESS: ....
NOTES:

ROLE: ☐ BACKGROUND CHECK
NAME: .... EMAIL: ....
PHONE: (......)................ ADDRESS: ....
NOTES:

VOLUNTEER CONTACT INFORMATION (CONTINUED)

ROLE: ☐ BACKGROUND CHECK
NAME: .... EMAIL: ....
PHONE: (......).................. ADDRESS: ....
NOTES:

ROLE: ☐ BACKGROUND CHECK
NAME: .... EMAIL: ....
PHONE: (......).................. ADDRESS: ....
NOTES:

ROLE: ☐ BACKGROUND CHECK
NAME: .... EMAIL: ....
PHONE: (......).................. ADDRESS: ....
NOTES:

ROLE: ☐ BACKGROUND CHECK
NAME: .... EMAIL: ....
PHONE: (......).................. ADDRESS: ....
NOTES:

ROLE: ☐ BACKGROUND CHECK
NAME: .... EMAIL: ....
PHONE: (......).................. ADDRESS: ....
NOTES:

SERVICE UNIT:

MEETING SCHEDULE: .... MEETING LOCATION: ....

POSITION:
- NAME: ....
- PHONE: (......) ....
- EMAIL: ....
- NOTES:

POSITION:
- NAME: ....
- PHONE: (......) ....
- EMAIL: ....
- NOTES:

POSITION:
- NAME: ....
- PHONE: (......) ....
- EMAIL: ....
- NOTES:

POSITION:
- NAME: ....
- PHONE: (......) ....
- EMAIL: ....
- NOTES:

POSITION:
- NAME: ....
- PHONE: (......) ....
- EMAIL: ....
- NOTES:

POSITION:
- NAME: ....
- PHONE: (......) ....
- EMAIL: ....
- NOTES:

POSITION:
- NAME: ....
- PHONE: (......) ....
- EMAIL: ....
- NOTES:

POSITION:
- NAME: ....
- PHONE: (......) ....
- EMAIL: ....
- NOTES:

COUNCIL:

PHONE: (....) .... FAX: (....) .... EMAIL(S): ....

SERVICE CENTER ADDRESS: .... SERVICE CENTER HOURS: ....

SHOP ADDRESS: .... SHOP HOURS: ....

WEBSITE: .... SOCIAL MEDIA: ....

NOTES:

POSITION:
NAME: ....
PHONE: (......) ....
EMAIL: ....
NOTES:

POSITION:
NAME: ....
PHONE: (......) ....
EMAIL: ....
NOTES:

POSITION:
NAME: ....
PHONE: (......) ....
EMAIL: ....
NOTES:

POSITION:
NAME: ....
PHONE: (......) ....
EMAIL: ....
NOTES:

POSITION:
NAME: ....
PHONE: (......) ....
EMAIL: ....
NOTES:

POSITION:
NAME: ....
PHONE: (......) ....
EMAIL: ....
NOTES:

TROOP ROSTER

GIRL: .... BIRTHDAY: ....../....../...... AGE: ......

PHONE: (......)................ EMAIL: .... SCHOOL: .... GRADE: ....

ADDRESS: .... LIVES WITH: ....

SHIRT SIZE: .... ALLERGIES: .... ON FILE: ☐ REGISTRATION ☐ HEALTH HISTORY ☐ ANNUAL PERMISSION SLIP ☐ OTHER: ....

PARENT/GUARDIAN: .... PHONE: (......)............. EMAIL: ....

PARENT/GUARDIAN: .... PHONE: (......)............. EMAIL: ....

NOTES:

☐ DAISY ☐ BROWNIE ☐ JUNIOR ☐ CADETTE ☐ SENIOR ☐ AMBASSADOR

GIRL: .... BIRTHDAY: ....../....../...... AGE: ......

PHONE: (......)................ EMAIL: .... SCHOOL: .... GRADE: ....

ADDRESS: .... LIVES WITH: ....

SHIRT SIZE: .... ALLERGIES: .... ON FILE: ☐ REGISTRATION ☐ HEALTH HISTORY ☐ ANNUAL PERMISSION SLIP ☐ OTHER: ....

PARENT/GUARDIAN: .... PHONE: (......)............. EMAIL: ....

PARENT/GUARDIAN: .... PHONE: (......)............. EMAIL: ....

NOTES:

☐ DAISY ☐ BROWNIE ☐ JUNIOR ☐ CADETTE ☐ SENIOR ☐ AMBASSADOR

GIRL: .... BIRTHDAY: ....../....../...... AGE: ......

PHONE: (......)................ EMAIL: .... SCHOOL: .... GRADE: ....

ADDRESS: .... LIVES WITH: ....

SHIRT SIZE: .... ALLERGIES: .... ON FILE: ☐ REGISTRATION ☐ HEALTH HISTORY ☐ ANNUAL PERMISSION SLIP ☐ OTHER: ....

PARENT/GUARDIAN: .... PHONE: (......)............. EMAIL: ....

PARENT/GUARDIAN: .... PHONE: (......)............. EMAIL: ....

NOTES:

☐ DAISY ☐ BROWNIE ☐ JUNIOR ☐ CADETTE ☐ SENIOR ☐ AMBASSADOR

TROOP ROSTER (CONTINUED)

GIRL: .... **BIRTHDAY:** ..../......../........ **AGE:** ....

PHONE: (........) .... **EMAIL:** .... **SCHOOL:** .... **GRADE:** ....

ADDRESS: .... **LIVES WITH:** ....

SHIRT SIZE: .... **ALLERGIES:** .... **ON FILE:** ☐ REGISTRATION ☐ HEALTH HISTORY ☐ ANNUAL PERMISSION SLIP ☐ OTHER: ....

PARENT/GUARDIAN: .... **PHONE:** (........) .... **EMAIL:** ....

PARENT/GUARDIAN: .... **PHONE:** (........) .... **EMAIL:** ....

NOTES: ....

☐ DAISY ☐ BROWNIE ☐ JUNIOR ☐ CADETTE ☐ SENIOR ☐ AMBASSADOR

GIRL: .... **BIRTHDAY:** ..../......../........ **AGE:** ....

PHONE: (........) .... **EMAIL:** .... **SCHOOL:** .... **GRADE:** ....

ADDRESS: .... **LIVES WITH:** ....

SHIRT SIZE: .... **ALLERGIES:** .... **ON FILE:** ☐ REGISTRATION ☐ HEALTH HISTORY ☐ ANNUAL PERMISSION SLIP ☐ OTHER: ....

PARENT/GUARDIAN: .... **PHONE:** (........) .... **EMAIL:** ....

PARENT/GUARDIAN: .... **PHONE:** (........) .... **EMAIL:** ....

NOTES: ....

☐ DAISY ☐ BROWNIE ☐ JUNIOR ☐ CADETTE ☐ SENIOR ☐ AMBASSADOR

GIRL: .... **BIRTHDAY:** ..../......../........ **AGE:** ....

PHONE: (........) .... **EMAIL:** .... **SCHOOL:** .... **GRADE:** ....

ADDRESS: .... **LIVES WITH:** ....

SHIRT SIZE: .... **ALLERGIES:** .... **ON FILE:** ☐ REGISTRATION ☐ HEALTH HISTORY ☐ ANNUAL PERMISSION SLIP ☐ OTHER: ....

PARENT/GUARDIAN: .... **PHONE:** (........) .... **EMAIL:** ....

PARENT/GUARDIAN: .... **PHONE:** (........) .... **EMAIL:** ....

NOTES: ....

☐ DAISY ☐ BROWNIE ☐ JUNIOR ☐ CADETTE ☐ SENIOR ☐ AMBASSADOR

"So often in life, things that you regard as an impediment turn out to be great good fortune."
— RUTH BADER GINSBURG

GIRL: .... **BIRTHDAY:** ....../....../...... **AGE:** ......

PHONE: (......)..................... **EMAIL:** .... **SCHOOL:** .... **GRADE:** ....

ADDRESS: .... **LIVES WITH:** ....

SHIRT SIZE: .... **ALLERGIES:** .... **ON FILE:** ☐ REGISTRATION ☐ HEALTH HISTORY ☐ ANNUAL PERMISSION SLIP ☐ OTHER: ....

PARENT/GUARDIAN: .... **PHONE:** (......)................ **EMAIL:** ....

PARENT/GUARDIAN: .... **PHONE:** (......)................ **EMAIL:** ....

NOTES:

☐ DAISY ☐ BROWNIE ☐ JUNIOR ☐ CADETTE ☐ SENIOR ☐ AMBASSADOR

GIRL: .... **BIRTHDAY:** ....../....../...... **AGE:** ......

PHONE: (......)..................... **EMAIL:** .... **SCHOOL:** .... **GRADE:** ....

ADDRESS: .... **LIVES WITH:** ....

SHIRT SIZE: .... **ALLERGIES:** .... **ON FILE:** ☐ REGISTRATION ☐ HEALTH HISTORY ☐ ANNUAL PERMISSION SLIP ☐ OTHER: ....

PARENT/GUARDIAN: .... **PHONE:** (......)................ **EMAIL:** ....

PARENT/GUARDIAN: .... **PHONE:** (......)................ **EMAIL:** ....

NOTES:

☐ DAISY ☐ BROWNIE ☐ JUNIOR ☐ CADETTE ☐ SENIOR ☐ AMBASSADOR

GIRL: .... **BIRTHDAY:** ....../....../...... **AGE:** ......

PHONE: (......)..................... **EMAIL:** .... **SCHOOL:** .... **GRADE:** ....

ADDRESS: .... **LIVES WITH:** ....

SHIRT SIZE: .... **ALLERGIES:** .... **ON FILE:** ☐ REGISTRATION ☐ HEALTH HISTORY ☐ ANNUAL PERMISSION SLIP ☐ OTHER: ....

PARENT/GUARDIAN: .... **PHONE:** (......)................ **EMAIL:** ....

PARENT/GUARDIAN: .... **PHONE:** (......)................ **EMAIL:** ....

NOTES:

☐ DAISY ☐ BROWNIE ☐ JUNIOR ☐ CADETTE ☐ SENIOR ☐ AMBASSADOR

TROOP ROSTER (CONTINUED)

GIRL: .... **BIRTHDAY:** ....../....../...... **AGE:** ......

PHONE: (......) .... **EMAIL:** .... **SCHOOL:** .... **GRADE:** ....

ADDRESS: .... **LIVES WITH:** ....

SHIRT SIZE: .... **ALLERGIES:** .... **ON FILE:** ☐ REGISTRATION ☐ HEALTH HISTORY ☐ ANNUAL PERMISSION SLIP ☐ OTHER: ....

PARENT/GUARDIAN: .... **PHONE:** (......) .... **EMAIL:** ....

PARENT/GUARDIAN: .... **PHONE:** (......) .... **EMAIL:** ....

NOTES:

☐ DAISY ☐ BROWNIE ☐ JUNIOR ☐ CADETTE ☐ SENIOR ☐ AMBASSADOR

GIRL: .... **BIRTHDAY:** ....../....../...... **AGE:** ......

PHONE: (......) .... **EMAIL:** .... **SCHOOL:** .... **GRADE:** ....

ADDRESS: .... **LIVES WITH:** ....

SHIRT SIZE: .... **ALLERGIES:** .... **ON FILE:** ☐ REGISTRATION ☐ HEALTH HISTORY ☐ ANNUAL PERMISSION SLIP ☐ OTHER: ....

PARENT/GUARDIAN: .... **PHONE:** (......) .... **EMAIL:** ....

PARENT/GUARDIAN: .... **PHONE:** (......) .... **EMAIL:** ....

NOTES:

☐ DAISY ☐ BROWNIE ☐ JUNIOR ☐ CADETTE ☐ SENIOR ☐ AMBASSADOR

GIRL: .... **BIRTHDAY:** ....../....../...... **AGE:** ......

PHONE: (......) .... **EMAIL:** .... **SCHOOL:** .... **GRADE:** ....

ADDRESS: .... **LIVES WITH:** ....

SHIRT SIZE: .... **ALLERGIES:** .... **ON FILE:** ☐ REGISTRATION ☐ HEALTH HISTORY ☐ ANNUAL PERMISSION SLIP ☐ OTHER: ....

PARENT/GUARDIAN: .... **PHONE:** (......) .... **EMAIL:** ....

PARENT/GUARDIAN: .... **PHONE:** (......) .... **EMAIL:** ....

NOTES:

☐ DAISY ☐ BROWNIE ☐ JUNIOR ☐ CADETTE ☐ SENIOR ☐ AMBASSADOR

"I attribute my success to this: I never gave or took an excuse."
FLORENCE NIGHTINGALE

GIRL: .... **BIRTHDAY:** ....../....../...... **AGE:** ......

PHONE: (......)............... **EMAIL:** .... **SCHOOL:** .... **GRADE:** ....

ADDRESS: .... **LIVES WITH:** ....

SHIRT SIZE: .... **ALLERGIES:** .... **ON FILE:** ☐ REGISTRATION ☐ HEALTH HISTORY ☐ ANNUAL PERMISSION SLIP ☐ OTHER: ....

PARENT/GUARDIAN: .... **PHONE:** (......)............... **EMAIL:** ....

PARENT/GUARDIAN: .... **PHONE:** (......)............... **EMAIL:** ....

NOTES:

☐ DAISY ☐ BROWNIE ☐ JUNIOR ☐ CADETTE ☐ SENIOR ☐ AMBASSADOR

GIRL: .... **BIRTHDAY:** ....../....../...... **AGE:** ......

PHONE: (......)............... **EMAIL:** .... **SCHOOL:** .... **GRADE:** ....

ADDRESS: .... **LIVES WITH:** ....

SHIRT SIZE: .... **ALLERGIES:** .... **ON FILE:** ☐ REGISTRATION ☐ HEALTH HISTORY ☐ ANNUAL PERMISSION SLIP ☐ OTHER: ....

PARENT/GUARDIAN: .... **PHONE:** (......)............... **EMAIL:** ....

PARENT/GUARDIAN: .... **PHONE:** (......)............... **EMAIL:** ....

NOTES:

☐ DAISY ☐ BROWNIE ☐ JUNIOR ☐ CADETTE ☐ SENIOR ☐ AMBASSADOR

GIRL: .... **BIRTHDAY:** ....../....../...... **AGE:** ......

PHONE: (......)............... **EMAIL:** .... **SCHOOL:** .... **GRADE:** ....

ADDRESS: .... **LIVES WITH:** ....

SHIRT SIZE: .... **ALLERGIES:** .... **ON FILE:** ☐ REGISTRATION ☐ HEALTH HISTORY ☐ ANNUAL PERMISSION SLIP ☐ OTHER: ....

PARENT/GUARDIAN: .... **PHONE:** (......)............... **EMAIL:** ....

PARENT/GUARDIAN: .... **PHONE:** (......)............... **EMAIL:** ....

NOTES:

☐ DAISY ☐ BROWNIE ☐ JUNIOR ☐ CADETTE ☐ SENIOR ☐ AMBASSADOR

TROOP ROSTER (CONTINUED)

GIRL: .... **BIRTHDAY:** ...../...../..... **AGE:** ......

PHONE: (......).................. **EMAIL:** .... **SCHOOL:** .... **GRADE:** ....

ADDRESS: .... **LIVES WITH:** ....

SHIRT SIZE: .... **ALLERGIES:** .... **ON FILE:** ☐ REGISTRATION ☐ HEALTH HISTORY ☐ ANNUAL PERMISSION SLIP ☐ OTHER: ....

PARENT/GUARDIAN: .... **PHONE:** (......)............ **EMAIL:** ....

PARENT/GUARDIAN: .... **PHONE:** (......)............ **EMAIL:** ....

NOTES:

☐ DAISY ☐ BROWNIE ☐ JUNIOR ☐ CADETTE ☐ SENIOR ☐ AMBASSADOR

GIRL: .... **BIRTHDAY:** ...../...../..... **AGE:** ......

PHONE: (......).................. **EMAIL:** .... **SCHOOL:** .... **GRADE:** ....

ADDRESS: .... **LIVES WITH:** ....

SHIRT SIZE: .... **ALLERGIES:** .... **ON FILE:** ☐ REGISTRATION ☐ HEALTH HISTORY ☐ ANNUAL PERMISSION SLIP ☐ OTHER: ....

PARENT/GUARDIAN: .... **PHONE:** (......)............ **EMAIL:** ....

PARENT/GUARDIAN: .... **PHONE:** (......)............ **EMAIL:** ....

NOTES:

☐ DAISY ☐ BROWNIE ☐ JUNIOR ☐ CADETTE ☐ SENIOR ☐ AMBASSADOR

GIRL: .... **BIRTHDAY:** ...../...../..... **AGE:** ......

PHONE: (......).................. **EMAIL:** .... **SCHOOL:** .... **GRADE:** ....

ADDRESS: .... **LIVES WITH:** ....

SHIRT SIZE: .... **ALLERGIES:** .... **ON FILE:** ☐ REGISTRATION ☐ HEALTH HISTORY ☐ ANNUAL PERMISSION SLIP ☐ OTHER: ....

PARENT/GUARDIAN: .... **PHONE:** (......)............ **EMAIL:** ....

PARENT/GUARDIAN: .... **PHONE:** (......)............ **EMAIL:** ....

NOTES:

☐ DAISY ☐ BROWNIE ☐ JUNIOR ☐ CADETTE ☐ SENIOR ☐ AMBASSADOR

"Make the most of yourself by fanning the tiny, inner sparks of possibility into flames of achievement."
GOLDA MEIR

GIRL: .... **BIRTHDAY:** ...... / ...... / ...... **AGE:** ......

PHONE: (......) .... **EMAIL:** .... **SCHOOL:** .... **GRADE:** ....

ADDRESS: .... **LIVES WITH:** ....

SHIRT SIZE: .... **ALLERGIES:** .... **ON FILE:** ☐ REGISTRATION ☐ HEALTH HISTORY ☐ ANNUAL PERMISSION SLIP ☐ OTHER: ....

PARENT/GUARDIAN: .... **PHONE:** (......) .... **EMAIL:** ....

PARENT/GUARDIAN: .... **PHONE:** (......) .... **EMAIL:** ....

NOTES:

☐ DAISY ☐ BROWNIE ☐ JUNIOR ☐ CADETTE ☐ SENIOR ☐ AMBASSADOR

GIRL: .... **BIRTHDAY:** ...... / ...... / ...... **AGE:** ......

PHONE: (......) .... **EMAIL:** .... **SCHOOL:** .... **GRADE:** ....

ADDRESS: .... **LIVES WITH:** ....

SHIRT SIZE: .... **ALLERGIES:** .... **ON FILE:** ☐ REGISTRATION ☐ HEALTH HISTORY ☐ ANNUAL PERMISSION SLIP ☐ OTHER: ....

PARENT/GUARDIAN: .... **PHONE:** (......) .... **EMAIL:** ....

PARENT/GUARDIAN: .... **PHONE:** (......) .... **EMAIL:** ....

NOTES:

☐ DAISY ☐ BROWNIE ☐ JUNIOR ☐ CADETTE ☐ SENIOR ☐ AMBASSADOR

GIRL: .... **BIRTHDAY:** ...... / ...... / ...... **AGE:** ......

PHONE: (......) .... **EMAIL:** .... **SCHOOL:** .... **GRADE:** ....

ADDRESS: .... **LIVES WITH:** ....

SHIRT SIZE: .... **ALLERGIES:** .... **ON FILE:** ☐ REGISTRATION ☐ HEALTH HISTORY ☐ ANNUAL PERMISSION SLIP ☐ OTHER: ....

PARENT/GUARDIAN: .... **PHONE:** (......) .... **EMAIL:** ....

PARENT/GUARDIAN: .... **PHONE:** (......) .... **EMAIL:** ....

NOTES:

☐ DAISY ☐ BROWNIE ☐ JUNIOR ☐ CADETTE ☐ SENIOR ☐ AMBASSADOR

TROOP ROSTER (CONTINUED)

GIRL: .... **BIRTHDAY:** ....../....../...... **AGE:** ......

PHONE: (......) .... **EMAIL:** .... **SCHOOL:** .... **GRADE:** ....

ADDRESS: .... **LIVES WITH:** ....

SHIRT SIZE: .... **ALLERGIES:** .... **ON FILE:** ☐ REGISTRATION ☐ HEALTH HISTORY ☐ ANNUAL PERMISSION SLIP ☐ OTHER: ....

PARENT/GUARDIAN: .... **PHONE:** (......) .... **EMAIL:** ....

PARENT/GUARDIAN: .... **PHONE:** (......) .... **EMAIL:** ....

NOTES:

☐ DAISY   ☐ BROWNIE   ☐ JUNIOR   ☐ CADETTE   ☐ SENIOR   ☐ AMBASSADOR

GIRL: .... **BIRTHDAY:** ....../....../...... **AGE:** ......

PHONE: (......) .... **EMAIL:** .... **SCHOOL:** .... **GRADE:** ....

ADDRESS: .... **LIVES WITH:** ....

SHIRT SIZE: .... **ALLERGIES:** .... **ON FILE:** ☐ REGISTRATION ☐ HEALTH HISTORY ☐ ANNUAL PERMISSION SLIP ☐ OTHER: ....

PARENT/GUARDIAN: .... **PHONE:** (......) .... **EMAIL:** ....

PARENT/GUARDIAN: .... **PHONE:** (......) .... **EMAIL:** ....

NOTES:

☐ DAISY   ☐ BROWNIE   ☐ JUNIOR   ☐ CADETTE   ☐ SENIOR   ☐ AMBASSADOR

GIRL: .... **BIRTHDAY:** ....../....../...... **AGE:** ......

PHONE: (......) .... **EMAIL:** .... **SCHOOL:** .... **GRADE:** ....

ADDRESS: .... **LIVES WITH:** ....

SHIRT SIZE: .... **ALLERGIES:** .... **ON FILE:** ☐ REGISTRATION ☐ HEALTH HISTORY ☐ ANNUAL PERMISSION SLIP ☐ OTHER: ....

PARENT/GUARDIAN: .... **PHONE:** (......) .... **EMAIL:** ....

PARENT/GUARDIAN: .... **PHONE:** (......) .... **EMAIL:** ....

NOTES:

☐ DAISY   ☐ BROWNIE   ☐ JUNIOR   ☐ CADETTE   ☐ SENIOR   ☐ AMBASSADOR

"The most difficult thing is the decision to act, the rest is merely tenacity."
— AMELIA EARHART

GIRL: .... **BIRTHDAY:** ....../....../...... **AGE:** ......

PHONE: (......) .... **EMAIL:** .... **SCHOOL:** .... **GRADE:** ....

ADDRESS: .... **LIVES WITH:** ....

SHIRT SIZE: .... **ALLERGIES:** .... **ON FILE:** ☐ REGISTRATION ☐ HEALTH HISTORY ☐ ANNUAL PERMISSION SLIP ☐ OTHER: ....

PARENT/GUARDIAN: .... **PHONE:** (......) .... **EMAIL:** ....

PARENT/GUARDIAN: .... **PHONE:** (......) .... **EMAIL:** ....

NOTES:

☐ DAISY ☐ BROWNIE ☐ JUNIOR ☐ CADETTE ☐ SENIOR ☐ AMBASSADOR

GIRL: .... **BIRTHDAY:** ....../....../...... **AGE:** ......

PHONE: (......) .... **EMAIL:** .... **SCHOOL:** .... **GRADE:** ....

ADDRESS: .... **LIVES WITH:** ....

SHIRT SIZE: .... **ALLERGIES:** .... **ON FILE:** ☐ REGISTRATION ☐ HEALTH HISTORY ☐ ANNUAL PERMISSION SLIP ☐ OTHER: ....

PARENT/GUARDIAN: .... **PHONE:** (......) .... **EMAIL:** ....

PARENT/GUARDIAN: .... **PHONE:** (......) .... **EMAIL:** ....

NOTES:

☐ DAISY ☐ BROWNIE ☐ JUNIOR ☐ CADETTE ☐ SENIOR ☐ AMBASSADOR

GIRL: .... **BIRTHDAY:** ....../....../...... **AGE:** ......

PHONE: (......) .... **EMAIL:** .... **SCHOOL:** .... **GRADE:** ....

ADDRESS: .... **LIVES WITH:** ....

SHIRT SIZE: .... **ALLERGIES:** .... **ON FILE:** ☐ REGISTRATION ☐ HEALTH HISTORY ☐ ANNUAL PERMISSION SLIP ☐ OTHER: ....

PARENT/GUARDIAN: .... **PHONE:** (......) .... **EMAIL:** ....

PARENT/GUARDIAN: .... **PHONE:** (......) .... **EMAIL:** ....

NOTES:

☐ DAISY ☐ BROWNIE ☐ JUNIOR ☐ CADETTE ☐ SENIOR ☐ AMBASSADOR

TROOP ROSTER (CONTINUED)

GIRL: .... **BIRTHDAY:** ....../....../...... **AGE:** ......

PHONE: (......) .... **EMAIL:** .... **SCHOOL:** .... **GRADE:** ....

ADDRESS: .... **LIVES WITH:** ....

SHIRT SIZE: .... **ALLERGIES:** .... **ON FILE:** ☐ REGISTRATION ☐ HEALTH HISTORY ☐ ANNUAL PERMISSION SLIP ☐ OTHER: ....

PARENT/GUARDIAN: .... **PHONE:** (......) .... **EMAIL:** ....

PARENT/GUARDIAN: .... **PHONE:** (......) .... **EMAIL:** ....

NOTES: ....

☐ DAISY ☐ BROWNIE ☐ JUNIOR ☐ CADETTE ☐ SENIOR ☐ AMBASSADOR

GIRL: .... **BIRTHDAY:** ....../....../...... **AGE:** ......

PHONE: (......) .... **EMAIL:** .... **SCHOOL:** .... **GRADE:** ....

ADDRESS: .... **LIVES WITH:** ....

SHIRT SIZE: .... **ALLERGIES:** .... **ON FILE:** ☐ REGISTRATION ☐ HEALTH HISTORY ☐ ANNUAL PERMISSION SLIP ☐ OTHER: ....

PARENT/GUARDIAN: .... **PHONE:** (......) .... **EMAIL:** ....

PARENT/GUARDIAN: .... **PHONE:** (......) .... **EMAIL:** ....

NOTES: ....

☐ DAISY ☐ BROWNIE ☐ JUNIOR ☐ CADETTE ☐ SENIOR ☐ AMBASSADOR

GIRL: .... **BIRTHDAY:** ....../....../...... **AGE:** ......

PHONE: (......) .... **EMAIL:** .... **SCHOOL:** .... **GRADE:** ....

ADDRESS: .... **LIVES WITH:** ....

SHIRT SIZE: .... **ALLERGIES:** .... **ON FILE:** ☐ REGISTRATION ☐ HEALTH HISTORY ☐ ANNUAL PERMISSION SLIP ☐ OTHER: ....

PARENT/GUARDIAN: .... **PHONE:** (......) .... **EMAIL:** ....

PARENT/GUARDIAN: .... **PHONE:** (......) .... **EMAIL:** ....

NOTES: ....

☐ DAISY ☐ BROWNIE ☐ JUNIOR ☐ CADETTE ☐ SENIOR ☐ AMBASSADOR

Troop Birthdays

January	February	March

April	May	June

July	August	September

October	November	December

YEAR AT-A-GLANCE

S M T W T F S	S M T W T F S	S M T W T F S

S M T W T F S	S M T W T F S	S M T W T F S

"The work of today is the history of tomorrow and we are its makers."
JULIETTE GORDON LOW

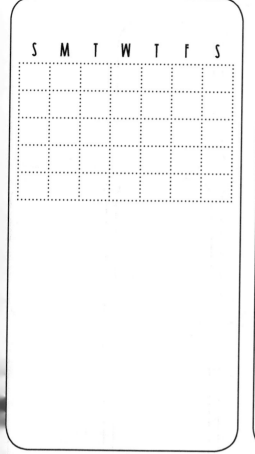
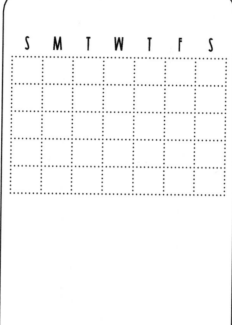
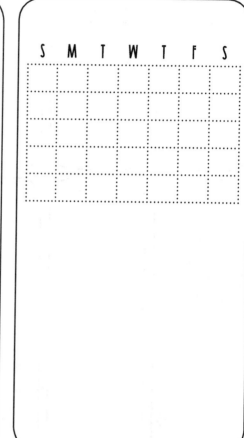
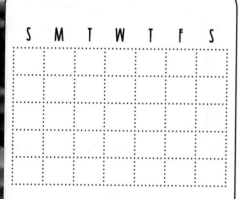
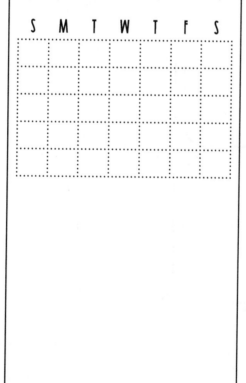

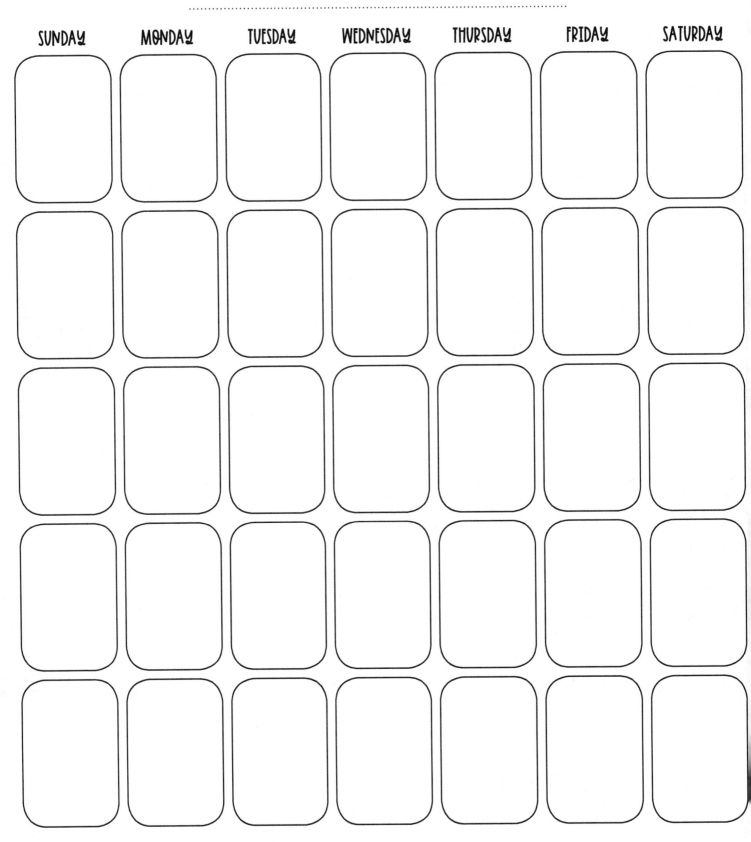

NOTES:

SUNDAY	MONDAY	TUESDAY	WEDNESDAY	THURSDAY	FRIDAY	SATURDAY

NOTES:

SUNDAY	MONDAY	TUESDAY	WEDNESDAY	THURSDAY	FRIDAY	SATURDAY

NOTES:

SUNDAY	MONDAY	TUESDAY	WEDNESDAY	THURSDAY	FRIDAY	SATURDAY

NOTES:

SUNDAY	MONDAY	TUESDAY	WEDNESDAY	THURSDAY	FRIDAY	SATURDAY

NOTES:

SUNDAY	MONDAY	TUESDAY	WEDNESDAY	THURSDAY	FRIDAY	SATURDAY

NOTES:

SUNDAY	MONDAY	TUESDAY	WEDNESDAY	THURSDAY	FRIDAY	SATURDAY

NOTES:

SUNDAY	MONDAY	TUESDAY	WEDNESDAY	THURSDAY	FRIDAY	SATURDAY

NOTES:

SUNDAY	MONDAY	TUESDAY	WEDNESDAY	THURSDAY	FRIDAY	SATURDAY

NOTES:

MEETING PLANNER

DATE:

MEETING DETAILS
TIME: .... LOCATION: .... BADGE/JOURNEY/AWARD: ....

MEETING GOAL/THEME: ....

PRE-MEETING PREP:

SUPPLIES:
- ☐
- ☐
- ☐
- ☐
- ☐

VOLUNTEERS:
- ☐
- ☐
- ☐
- ☐
- ☐

REMINDERS:

MEETING STRUCTURE:

START-UP ACTIVITY:

___

OPENING:

___

BUSINESS:

___

ACTIVITIES:

(1)

(2)

(3)

(4)

(5)

___

CLEAN-UP & CLOSING:

NEXT MEETING:

REFLECTION:

DURING THIS MEETING, THE GIRLS...
☐ DISCOVERED ☐ CONNECTED ☐ TOOK ACTION

OUR ACTIVITIES WERE...
☐ GIRL-LED ☐ HANDS-ON ☐ COOPERATIVE

ATTENDANCE:
LOW ○ ○ ○ ○ ○ HIGH

ENJOYMENT:
LOW ○ ○ ○ ○ ○ HIGH

ENGAGEMENT:
LOW ○ ○ ○ ○ ○ HIGH

WHAT WAS MOST SUCCESSFUL?

WHAT COULD IMPROVE?

MEETING PLANNER

DATE:

MEETING DETAILS

TIME: .... LOCATION: .... BADGE/JOURNEY/AWARD: ....

MEETING GOAL/THEME: ....

PRE-MEETING PREP:

SUPPLIES:
- ☐
- ☐
- ☐
- ☐
- ☐

VOLUNTEERS:
- ☐
- ☐
- ☐
- ☐
- ☐

REMINDERS:

MEETING STRUCTURE:

START-UP ACTIVITY:

OPENING:

BUSINESS:

ACTIVITIES:

(1)

(2)

(3)

(4)

(5)

CLEAN-UP & CLOSING:

NEXT MEETING:

REFLECTION:

DURING THIS MEETING, THE GIRLS...
☐ DISCOVERED ☐ CONNECTED ☐ TOOK ACTION

OUR ACTIVITIES WERE...
☐ GIRL-LED ☐ HANDS-ON ☐ COOPERATIVE

ATTENDANCE:
LOW ○ ○ ○ ○ ○ HIGH

ENJOYMENT:
LOW ○ ○ ○ ○ ○ HIGH

ENGAGEMENT:
LOW ○ ○ ○ ○ ○ HIGH

WHAT WAS MOST SUCCESSFUL?

WHAT COULD IMPROVE?

MEETING PLANNER

DATE:

MEETING DETAILS
TIME: .... LOCATION: .... BADGE/JOURNEY/AWARD: ....

MEETING GOAL/THEME: ....

PRE-MEETING PREP:

SUPPLIES:
- ☐
- ☐
- ☐
- ☐
- ☐

VOLUNTEERS:
- ☐
- ☐
- ☐
- ☐
- ☐

REMINDERS:

MEETING STRUCTURE:

START-UP ACTIVITY:

_____

OPENING:

_____

BUSINESS:

_____

ACTIVITIES:

(1)

(2)

(3)

(4)

(5)

_____

CLEAN-UP & CLOSING:

NEXT MEETING:

REFLECTION:

DURING THIS MEETING, THE GIRLS...
☐ DISCOVERED ☐ CONNECTED ☐ TOOK ACTION

OUR ACTIVITIES WERE...
☐ GIRL-LED ☐ HANDS-ON ☐ COOPERATIVE

ATTENDANCE:
LOW ○ ○ ○ ○ ○ HIGH

ENJOYMENT:
LOW ○ ○ ○ ○ ○ HIGH

ENGAGEMENT:
LOW ○ ○ ○ ○ ○ HIGH

WHAT WAS MOST SUCCESSFUL?

WHAT COULD IMPROVE?

MEETING PLANNER

DATE:

MEETING DETAILS

TIME: .... LOCATION: .... BADGE/JOURNEY/AWARD: ....

MEETING GOAL/THEME: ....

PRE-MEETING PREP:

SUPPLIES:
- ☐
- ☐
- ☐
- ☐
- ☐
- ☐

VOLUNTEERS:
- ☐
- ☐
- ☐
- ☐
- ☐
- ☐

REMINDERS:

MEETING STRUCTURE:

START-UP ACTIVITY:

OPENING:

BUSINESS:

ACTIVITIES:

(1)

(2)

(3)

(4)

(5)

CLEAN-UP & CLOSING:

NEXT MEETING:

REFLECTION:

DURING THIS MEETING, THE GIRLS...
☐ DISCOVERED ☐ CONNECTED ☐ TOOK ACTION

OUR ACTIVITIES WERE...
☐ GIRL-LED ☐ HANDS-ON ☐ COOPERATIVE

ATTENDANCE:
LOW ○ ○ ○ ○ ○ HIGH

ENJOYMENT:
LOW ○ ○ ○ ○ ○ HIGH

ENGAGEMENT:
LOW ○ ○ ○ ○ ○ HIGH

WHAT WAS MOST SUCCESSFUL?

WHAT COULD IMPROVE?

MEETING PLANNER

DATE:

MEETING DETAILS

TIME: .... LOCATION: .... BADGE/JOURNEY/AWARD: ....

MEETING GOAL/THEME: ....

PRE-MEETING PREP:

SUPPLIES:
- ☐
- ☐
- ☐
- ☐
- ☐

VOLUNTEERS:
- ☐
- ☐
- ☐
- ☐
- ☐

REMINDERS:

MEETING STRUCTURE:

START-UP ACTIVITY:

OPENING:

BUSINESS:

ACTIVITIES:

(1)

(2)

(3)

(4)

(5)

CLEAN-UP & CLOSING:

NEXT MEETING:

REFLECTION:

DURING THIS MEETING, THE GIRLS...
☐ DISCOVERED ☐ CONNECTED ☐ TOOK ACTION

OUR ACTIVITIES WERE...
☐ GIRL-LED ☐ HANDS-ON ☐ COOPERATIVE

ATTENDANCE:
LOW ○ ○ ○ ○ ○ HIGH

ENJOYMENT:
LOW ○ ○ ○ ○ ○ HIGH

ENGAGEMENT:
LOW ○ ○ ○ ○ ○ HIGH

WHAT WAS MOST SUCCESSFUL?

WHAT COULD IMPROVE?

MEETING PLANNER

DATE:

MEETING DETAILS

TIME: .... LOCATION: .... BADGE/JOURNEY/AWARD: ....

MEETING GOAL/THEME: ....

PRE-MEETING PREP:

SUPPLIES:
- ☐
- ☐
- ☐
- ☐
- ☐
- ☐

VOLUNTEERS:
- ☐
- ☐
- ☐
- ☐
- ☐

REMINDERS:

MEETING STRUCTURE:

START-UP ACTIVITY:

OPENING:

BUSINESS:

ACTIVITIES:

(1)

(2)

(3)

(4)

(5)

CLEAN-UP & CLOSING:

NEXT MEETING:

REFLECTION:

DURING THIS MEETING, THE GIRLS...
☐ DISCOVERED ☐ CONNECTED ☐ TOOK ACTION

OUR ACTIVITIES WERE...
☐ GIRL-LED ☐ HANDS-ON ☐ COOPERATIVE

ATTENDANCE:
LOW ○ ○ ○ ○ ○ HIGH

ENJOYMENT:
LOW ○ ○ ○ ○ ○ HIGH

ENGAGEMENT:
LOW ○ ○ ○ ○ ○ HIGH

WHAT WAS MOST SUCCESSFUL?

WHAT COULD IMPROVE?

MEETING PLANNER

DATE:

MEETING DETAILS
TIME: .... LOCATION: .... BADGE/JOURNEY/AWARD: ....

MEETING GOAL/THEME: ....

PRE-MEETING PREP:

SUPPLIES:
- ☐
- ☐
- ☐
- ☐
- ☐

VOLUNTEERS:
- ☐
- ☐
- ☐
- ☐
- ☐

REMINDERS:

MEETING STRUCTURE:

START-UP ACTIVITY:

_____

OPENING:

_____

BUSINESS:

_____

ACTIVITIES:

(1)

(2)

(3)

(4)

(5)

_____

CLEAN-UP & CLOSING:

NEXT MEETING:

REFLECTION:

DURING THIS MEETING, THE GIRLS...
☐ DISCOVERED ☐ CONNECTED ☐ TOOK ACTION

OUR ACTIVITIES WERE...
☐ GIRL-LED   ☐ HANDS-ON ☐ COOPERATIVE

ATTENDANCE:
LOW ○ ○ ○ ○ ○ HIGH

ENJOYMENT:
LOW ○ ○ ○ ○ ○ HIGH

ENGAGEMENT:
LOW ○ ○ ○ ○ ○ HIGH

WHAT WAS MOST SUCCESSFUL?

WHAT COULD IMPROVE?

MEETING PLANNER

DATE:

MEETING DETAILS
TIME: .... LOCATION: .... BADGE/JOURNEY/AWARD: ....
MEETING GOAL/THEME: ....

PRE-MEETING PREP:

SUPPLIES:
- ☐
- ☐
- ☐
- ☐
- ☐

VOLUNTEERS:
- ☐
- ☐
- ☐
- ☐
- ☐

REMINDERS:

MEETING STRUCTURE:

START-UP ACTIVITY:

OPENING:

BUSINESS:

ACTIVITIES:

(1)

(2)

(3)

(4)

(5)

CLEAN-UP & CLOSING:

NEXT MEETING:

REFLECTION:

DURING THIS MEETING, THE GIRLS...
☐ DISCOVERED ☐ CONNECTED ☐ TOOK ACTION

OUR ACTIVITIES WERE...
☐ GIRL-LED ☐ HANDS-ON ☐ COOPERATIVE

ATTENDANCE:
LOW ○ ○ ○ ○ ○ HIGH

ENJOYMENT:
LOW ○ ○ ○ ○ ○ HIGH

ENGAGEMENT:
LOW ○ ○ ○ ○ ○ HIGH

WHAT WAS MOST SUCCESSFUL?

WHAT COULD IMPROVE?

MEETING PLANNER

DATE:

MEETING DETAILS

TIME: .... LOCATION: .... BADGE/JOURNEY/AWARD: ....

MEETING GOAL/THEME: ....

PRE-MEETING PREP:

SUPPLIES:
- ☐
- ☐
- ☐
- ☐
- ☐

VOLUNTEERS:
- ☐
- ☐
- ☐
- ☐
- ☐

REMINDERS:

MEETING STRUCTURE:

START-UP ACTIVITY:

___

OPENING:

___

BUSINESS:

___

ACTIVITIES:

(1)

(2)

(3)

(4)

(5)

___

CLEAN-UP & CLOSING:

NEXT MEETING:

REFLECTION:

DURING THIS MEETING, THE GIRLS...
☐ DISCOVERED ☐ CONNECTED ☐ TOOK ACTION

OUR ACTIVITIES WERE...
☐ GIRL-LED ☐ HANDS-ON ☐ COOPERATIVE

ATTENDANCE:
LOW ○ ○ ○ ○ ○ HIGH

ENJOYMENT:
LOW ○ ○ ○ ○ ○ HIGH

ENGAGEMENT:
LOW ○ ○ ○ ○ ○ HIGH

WHAT WAS MOST SUCCESSFUL?

WHAT COULD IMPROVE?

MEETING PLANNER

DATE:

MEETING DETAILS

TIME: .... LOCATION: .... BADGE/JOURNEY/AWARD: ....

MEETING GOAL/THEME: ....

PRE-MEETING PREP:

SUPPLIES:
- ☐
- ☐
- ☐
- ☐
- ☐

VOLUNTEERS:
- ☐
- ☐
- ☐
- ☐
- ☐

REMINDERS:

MEETING STRUCTURE:

START-UP ACTIVITY:

_____

OPENING:

_____

BUSINESS:

_____

ACTIVITIES:

(1)

(2)

(3)

(4)

(5)

_____

CLEAN-UP & CLOSING:

NEXT MEETING:

REFLECTION:

DURING THIS MEETING, THE GIRLS...
☐ DISCOVERED ☐ CONNECTED ☐ TOOK ACTION

OUR ACTIVITIES WERE...
☐ GIRL-LED ☐ HANDS-ON ☐ COOPERATIVE

ATTENDANCE:
LOW ○ ○ ○ ○ ○ HIGH

ENJOYMENT:
LOW ○ ○ ○ ○ ○ HIGH

ENGAGEMENT:
LOW ○ ○ ○ ○ ○ HIGH

WHAT WAS MOST SUCCESSFUL?

WHAT COULD IMPROVE?

MEETING PLANNER

DATE:

MEETING DETAILS
TIME: .... LOCATION: .... BADGE/JOURNEY/AWARD: ....

MEETING GOAL/THEME: ....

PRE-MEETING PREP:

SUPPLIES:
- ☐
- ☐
- ☐
- ☐
- ☐

VOLUNTEERS:
- ☐
- ☐
- ☐
- ☐
- ☐

REMINDERS:

MEETING STRUCTURE:

START-UP ACTIVITY:
_____

OPENING:
_____

BUSINESS:

_____

ACTIVITIES:

(1)

(2)

(3)

(4)

(5)
_____
CLEAN-UP & CLOSING:

NEXT MEETING:

REFLECTION:

DURING THIS MEETING, THE GIRLS...
☐ DISCOVERED ☐ CONNECTED ☐ TOOK ACTION

OUR ACTIVITIES WERE...
☐ GIRL-LED ☐ HANDS-ON ☐ COOPERATIVE

ATTENDANCE:
LOW ○ ○ ○ ○ ○ HIGH

ENJOYMENT:
LOW ○ ○ ○ ○ ○ HIGH

ENGAGEMENT:
LOW ○ ○ ○ ○ ○ HIGH

WHAT WAS MOST SUCCESSFUL?

WHAT COULD IMPROVE?

MEETING PLANNER

DATE:

MEETING DETAILS
TIME: .... LOCATION: .... BADGE/JOURNEY/AWARD: ....

MEETING GOAL/THEME: ....

PRE-MEETING PREP:

SUPPLIES:
- ☐
- ☐
- ☐
- ☐
- ☐

VOLUNTEERS:
- ☐
- ☐
- ☐
- ☐
- ☐

REMINDERS:

MEETING STRUCTURE:

START-UP ACTIVITY:

OPENING:

BUSINESS:

ACTIVITIES:

(1)

(2)

(3)

(4)

(5)

CLEAN-UP & CLOSING:

NEXT MEETING:

REFLECTION:

DURING THIS MEETING, THE GIRLS...
☐ DISCOVERED ☐ CONNECTED ☐ TOOK ACTION

OUR ACTIVITIES WERE...
☐ GIRL-LED ☐ HANDS-ON ☐ COOPERATIVE

ATTENDANCE:
LOW ○ ○ ○ ○ ○ HIGH

ENJOYMENT:
LOW ○ ○ ○ ○ ○ HIGH

ENGAGEMENT:
LOW ○ ○ ○ ○ ○ HIGH

WHAT WAS MOST SUCCESSFUL?

WHAT COULD IMPROVE?

MEETING PLANNER

DATE:

MEETING DETAILS

TIME: .... LOCATION: .... BADGE/JOURNEY/AWARD: ....

MEETING GOAL/THEME: ....

PRE-MEETING PREP:

SUPPLIES:
- [ ]
- [ ]
- [ ]
- [ ]
- [ ]

VOLUNTEERS:
- [ ]
- [ ]
- [ ]
- [ ]
- [ ]

REMINDERS:

MEETING STRUCTURE:

START-UP ACTIVITY:
_____

OPENING:
_____

BUSINESS:

_____

ACTIVITIES:

(1)

(2)

(3)

(4)

(5)
_____

CLEAN-UP & CLOSING:

NEXT MEETING:

REFLECTION:

DURING THIS MEETING, THE GIRLS...
- [ ] DISCOVERED - [ ] CONNECTED - [ ] TOOK ACTION

OUR ACTIVITIES WERE...
- [ ] GIRL-LED - [ ] HANDS-ON - [ ] COOPERATIVE

ATTENDANCE:
LOW ○ ○ ○ ○ ○ HIGH

ENJOYMENT:
LOW ○ ○ ○ ○ ○ HIGH

ENGAGEMENT:
LOW ○ ○ ○ ○ ○ HIGH

WHAT WAS MOST SUCCESSFUL?

WHAT COULD IMPROVE?

MEETING PLANNER

DATE:

MEETING DETAILS
TIME: .... LOCATION: .... BADGE/JOURNEY/AWARD: ....

MEETING GOAL/THEME: ....

PRE-MEETING PREP:

SUPPLIES:
- ☐
- ☐
- ☐
- ☐
- ☐

VOLUNTEERS:
- ☐
- ☐
- ☐
- ☐
- ☐

REMINDERS:

MEETING STRUCTURE:

START-UP ACTIVITY:

OPENING:

BUSINESS:

ACTIVITIES:

(1)

(2)

(3)

(4)

(5)

CLEAN-UP & CLOSING:

NEXT MEETING:

REFLECTION:

DURING THIS MEETING, THE GIRLS...
☐ DISCOVERED ☐ CONNECTED ☐ TOOK ACTION

OUR ACTIVITIES WERE...
☐ GIRL-LED ☐ HANDS-ON ☐ COOPERATIVE

ATTENDANCE:
LOW ○ ○ ○ ○ ○ HIGH

ENJOYMENT:
LOW ○ ○ ○ ○ ○ HIGH

ENGAGEMENT:
LOW ○ ○ ○ ○ ○ HIGH

WHAT WAS MOST SUCCESSFUL?

WHAT COULD IMPROVE?

MEETING PLANNER

DATE:

MEETING DETAILS

TIME: .... LOCATION: .... BADGE/JOURNEY/AWARD: ....

MEETING GOAL/THEME: ....

PRE-MEETING PREP:

SUPPLIES:
- ☐
- ☐
- ☐
- ☐
- ☐

VOLUNTEERS:
- ☐
- ☐
- ☐
- ☐
- ☐

REMINDERS:

MEETING STRUCTURE:

START-UP ACTIVITY:

___

OPENING:

___

BUSINESS:

___

ACTIVITIES:

(1)

(2)

(3)

(4)

(5)

___

CLEAN-UP & CLOSING:

NEXT MEETING:

REFLECTION:

DURING THIS MEETING, THE GIRLS...
☐ DISCOVERED ☐ CONNECTED ☐ TOOK ACTION

OUR ACTIVITIES WERE...
☐ GIRL-LED ☐ HANDS-ON ☐ COOPERATIVE

ATTENDANCE:
LOW ○ ○ ○ ○ ○ HIGH

ENJOYMENT:
LOW ○ ○ ○ ○ ○ HIGH

ENGAGEMENT:
LOW ○ ○ ○ ○ ○ HIGH

WHAT WAS MOST SUCCESSFUL?

WHAT COULD IMPROVE?

MEETING PLANNER

DATE:

MEETING DETAILS
TIME: .... LOCATION: .... BADGE/JOURNEY/AWARD: ....
MEETING GOAL/THEME: ....

PRE-MEETING PREP:

SUPPLIES:
- ☐
- ☐
- ☐
- ☐
- ☐

VOLUNTEERS:
- ☐
- ☐
- ☐
- ☐
- ☐

REMINDERS:

MEETING STRUCTURE:

START-UP ACTIVITY:

_____

OPENING:

_____

BUSINESS:

_____

ACTIVITIES:

(1)

(2)

(3)

(4)

(5)

_____

CLEAN-UP & CLOSING:

NEXT MEETING:

REFLECTION:

DURING THIS MEETING, THE GIRLS...
☐ DISCOVERED ☐ CONNECTED ☐ TOOK ACTION

OUR ACTIVITIES WERE...
☐ GIRL-LED ☐ HANDS-ON ☐ COOPERATIVE

ATTENDANCE:
LOW ○ ○ ○ ○ ○ HIGH

ENJOYMENT:
LOW ○ ○ ○ ○ ○ HIGH

ENGAGEMENT:
LOW ○ ○ ○ ○ ○ HIGH

WHAT WAS MOST SUCCESSFUL?

WHAT COULD IMPROVE?

MEETING PLANNER

DATE:

MEETING DETAILS
TIME: .... LOCATION: .... BADGE/JOURNEY/AWARD: ....

MEETING GOAL/THEME: ....

PRE-MEETING PREP:

SUPPLIES:
- ☐
- ☐
- ☐
- ☐
- ☐

VOLUNTEERS:
- ☐
- ☐
- ☐
- ☐
- ☐

REMINDERS:

MEETING STRUCTURE:

START-UP ACTIVITY:

_____

OPENING:

_____

BUSINESS:

_____

ACTIVITIES:

(1)

(2)

(3)

(4)

(5)

_____

CLEAN-UP & CLOSING:

NEXT MEETING:

REFLECTION:

DURING THIS MEETING, THE GIRLS...
☐ DISCOVERED ☐ CONNECTED ☐ TOOK ACTION

OUR ACTIVITIES WERE...
☐ GIRL-LED ☐ HANDS-ON ☐ COOPERATIVE

ATTENDANCE:
LOW ○ ○ ○ ○ ○ HIGH

ENJOYMENT:
LOW ○ ○ ○ ○ ○ HIGH

ENGAGEMENT:
LOW ○ ○ ○ ○ ○ HIGH

WHAT WAS MOST SUCCESSFUL?

WHAT COULD IMPROVE?

MEETING PLANNER   DATE:

MEETING DETAILS
TIME: .... LOCATION: .... BADGE/JOURNEY/AWARD: ....

MEETING GOAL/THEME: ....

PRE-MEETING PREP:

SUPPLIES:
- ☐
- ☐
- ☐
- ☐
- ☐
- ☐

VOLUNTEERS:
- ☐
- ☐
- ☐
- ☐
- ☐
- ☐

REMINDERS:

MEETING STRUCTURE:

START-UP ACTIVITY:

_____

OPENING:

_____

BUSINESS:

_____

ACTIVITIES:

(1)

(2)

(3)

(4)

(5)

_____

CLEAN-UP & CLOSING:

NEXT MEETING:

REFLECTION:

DURING THIS MEETING, THE GIRLS...
☐ DISCOVERED ☐ CONNECTED ☐ TOOK ACTION

OUR ACTIVITIES WERE...
☐ GIRL-LED ☐ HANDS-ON ☐ COOPERATIVE

ATTENDANCE:
LOW ○ ○ ○ ○ ○ HIGH

ENJOYMENT:
LOW ○ ○ ○ ○ ○ HIGH

ENGAGEMENT:
LOW ○ ○ ○ ○ ○ HIGH

WHAT WAS MOST SUCCESSFUL?

WHAT COULD IMPROVE?

MEETING PLANNER

DATE:

MEETING DETAILS

TIME: .... LOCATION: .... BADGE/JOURNEY/AWARD: ....

MEETING GOAL/THEME: ....

PRE-MEETING PREP:

SUPPLIES:
- ☐
- ☐
- ☐
- ☐
- ☐

VOLUNTEERS:
- ☐
- ☐
- ☐
- ☐
- ☐

REMINDERS:

MEETING STRUCTURE:

START-UP ACTIVITY:

___

OPENING:

___

BUSINESS:

___

ACTIVITIES:

(1)

(2)

(3)

(4)

(5)

___

CLEAN-UP & CLOSING:

NEXT MEETING:

REFLECTION:

DURING THIS MEETING, THE GIRLS...
☐ DISCOVERED ☐ CONNECTED ☐ TOOK ACTION

OUR ACTIVITIES WERE...
☐ GIRL-LED ☐ HANDS-ON ☐ COOPERATIVE

ATTENDANCE:
LOW ○ ○ ○ ○ ○ HIGH

ENJOYMENT:
LOW ○ ○ ○ ○ ○ HIGH

ENGAGEMENT:
LOW ○ ○ ○ ○ ○ HIGH

WHAT WAS MOST SUCCESSFUL?

WHAT COULD IMPROVE?

MEETING PLANNER   DATE:

MEETING DETAILS
TIME: .... LOCATION: .... BADGE/JOURNEY/AWARD: ....

MEETING GOAL/THEME: ....

PRE-MEETING PREP:

SUPPLIES:
- ☐
- ☐
- ☐
- ☐
- ☐

VOLUNTEERS:
- ☐
- ☐
- ☐
- ☐
- ☐

REMINDERS:

MEETING STRUCTURE:

START-UP ACTIVITY:
_____

OPENING:
_____

BUSINESS:
_____
_____

ACTIVITIES:

(1)

(2)

(3)

(4)

(5)
_____

CLEAN-UP & CLOSING:

NEXT MEETING:

REFLECTION:

DURING THIS MEETING, THE GIRLS...
☐ DISCOVERED ☐ CONNECTED ☐ TOOK ACTION

OUR ACTIVITIES WERE...
☐ GIRL-LED ☐ HANDS-ON ☐ COOPERATIVE

ATTENDANCE:
LOW ○ ○ ○ ○ ○ HIGH

ENJOYMENT:
LOW ○ ○ ○ ○ ○ HIGH

ENGAGEMENT:
LOW ○ ○ ○ ○ ○ HIGH

WHAT WAS MOST SUCCESSFUL?

WHAT COULD IMPROVE?

MEETING PLANNER

DATE:

MEETING DETAILS
TIME: .... LOCATION: .... BADGE/JOURNEY/AWARD: ....

MEETING GOAL/THEME: ....

PRE-MEETING PREP:

SUPPLIES:
- ☐
- ☐
- ☐
- ☐
- ☐

VOLUNTEERS:
- ☐
- ☐
- ☐
- ☐
- ☐

REMINDERS:

MEETING STRUCTURE:

START-UP ACTIVITY:

OPENING:

BUSINESS:

ACTIVITIES:

(1)

(2)

(3)

(4)

(5)

CLEAN-UP & CLOSING:

NEXT MEETING:

REFLECTION:

DURING THIS MEETING, THE GIRLS...
☐ DISCOVERED ☐ CONNECTED ☐ TOOK ACTION

OUR ACTIVITIES WERE...
☐ GIRL-LED ☐ HANDS-ON ☐ COOPERATIVE

ATTENDANCE:
LOW ○ ○ ○ ○ ○ HIGH

ENJOYMENT:
LOW ○ ○ ○ ○ ○ HIGH

ENGAGEMENT:
LOW ○ ○ ○ ○ ○ HIGH

WHAT WAS MOST SUCCESSFUL?

WHAT COULD IMPROVE?

MEETING PLANNER

DATE:

MEETING DETAILS
TIME: .... LOCATION: .... BADGE/JOURNEY/AWARD: ....

MEETING GOAL/THEME: ....

PRE-MEETING PREP:

SUPPLIES:
- ☐
- ☐
- ☐
- ☐
- ☐

VOLUNTEERS:
- ☐
- ☐
- ☐
- ☐
- ☐

REMINDERS:

MEETING STRUCTURE:

START-UP ACTIVITY:

_____

OPENING:

_____

BUSINESS:

_____

ACTIVITIES:

(1)

(2)

(3)

(4)

(5)

_____

CLEAN-UP & CLOSING:

NEXT MEETING:

REFLECTION:

DURING THIS MEETING, THE GIRLS...
☐ DISCOVERED ☐ CONNECTED ☐ TOOK ACTION

OUR ACTIVITIES WERE...
☐ GIRL-LED ☐ HANDS-ON ☐ COOPERATIVE

ATTENDANCE:
LOW ○ ○ ○ ○ ○ HIGH

ENJOYMENT:
LOW ○ ○ ○ ○ ○ HIGH

ENGAGEMENT:
LOW ○ ○ ○ ○ ○ HIGH

WHAT WAS MOST SUCCESSFUL?

WHAT COULD IMPROVE?

MEETING PLANNER

DATE:

MEETING DETAILS
TIME: .... LOCATION: .... BADGE/JOURNEY/AWARD: ....

MEETING GOAL/THEME: ....

PRE-MEETING PREP:

SUPPLIES:
- ☐
- ☐
- ☐
- ☐
- ☐

VOLUNTEERS:
- ☐
- ☐
- ☐
- ☐
- ☐

REMINDERS:

MEETING STRUCTURE:

START-UP ACTIVITY:

OPENING:

BUSINESS:

ACTIVITIES:

(1)

(2)

(3)

(4)

(5)

CLEAN-UP & CLOSING:

NEXT MEETING:

REFLECTION:

DURING THIS MEETING, THE GIRLS...
☐ DISCOVERED ☐ CONNECTED ☐ TOOK ACTION

OUR ACTIVITIES WERE...
☐ GIRL-LED ☐ HANDS-ON ☐ COOPERATIVE

ATTENDANCE:
LOW ○ ○ ○ ○ ○ HIGH

ENJOYMENT:
LOW ○ ○ ○ ○ ○ HIGH

ENGAGEMENT:
LOW ○ ○ ○ ○ ○ HIGH

WHAT WAS MOST SUCCESSFUL?

WHAT COULD IMPROVE?

MEETING PLANNER

DATE:

MEETING DETAILS
TIME: .... LOCATION: .... BADGE/JOURNEY/AWARD: ....

MEETING GOAL/THEME: ....

PRE-MEETING PREP:

SUPPLIES:
- ☐
- ☐
- ☐
- ☐
- ☐
- ☐

VOLUNTEERS:
- ☐
- ☐
- ☐
- ☐
- ☐

REMINDERS:

MEETING STRUCTURE:

START-UP ACTIVITY:

OPENING:

BUSINESS:

ACTIVITIES:

(1)

(2)

(3)

(4)

(5)

CLEAN-UP & CLOSING:

NEXT MEETING:

REFLECTION:

DURING THIS MEETING, THE GIRLS...
☐ DISCOVERED ☐ CONNECTED ☐ TOOK ACTION

OUR ACTIVITIES WERE...
☐ GIRL-LED ☐ HANDS-ON ☐ COOPERATIVE

ATTENDANCE:
LOW ○ ○ ○ ○ ○ HIGH

ENJOYMENT:
LOW ○ ○ ○ ○ ○ HIGH

ENGAGEMENT:
LOW ○ ○ ○ ○ ○ HIGH

WHAT WAS MOST SUCCESSFUL?

WHAT COULD IMPROVE?

MEETING PLANNER

DATE:

MEETING DETAILS

TIME: .... LOCATION: .... BADGE/JOURNEY/AWARD: ....

MEETING GOAL/THEME: ....

PRE-MEETING PREP:

SUPPLIES:
- ☐
- ☐
- ☐
- ☐
- ☐

VOLUNTEERS:
- ☐
- ☐
- ☐
- ☐
- ☐

REMINDERS:

MEETING STRUCTURE:

START-UP ACTIVITY:

OPENING:

BUSINESS:

ACTIVITIES:

(1)

(2)

(3)

(4)

(5)

CLEAN-UP & CLOSING:

NEXT MEETING:

REFLECTION:

DURING THIS MEETING, THE GIRLS...
☐ DISCOVERED ☐ CONNECTED ☐ TOOK ACTION

OUR ACTIVITIES WERE...
☐ GIRL-LED ☐ HANDS-ON ☐ COOPERATIVE

ATTENDANCE:
LOW ○ ○ ○ ○ ○ HIGH

ENJOYMENT:
LOW ○ ○ ○ ○ ○ HIGH

ENGAGEMENT:
LOW ○ ○ ○ ○ ○ HIGH

WHAT WAS MOST SUCCESSFUL?

WHAT COULD IMPROVE?

MEETING PLANNER

DATE:

MEETING DETAILS
TIME: .... LOCATION: .... BADGE/JOURNEY/AWARD: ....

MEETING GOAL/THEME: ....

PRE-MEETING PREP:

SUPPLIES:
- ☐
- ☐
- ☐
- ☐
- ☐

VOLUNTEERS:
- ☐
- ☐
- ☐
- ☐
- ☐

REMINDERS:

MEETING STRUCTURE:

START-UP ACTIVITY:

OPENING:

BUSINESS:

ACTIVITIES:

(1)

(2)

(3)

(4)

(5)

CLEAN-UP & CLOSING:

NEXT MEETING:

REFLECTION:

DURING THIS MEETING, THE GIRLS...
☐ DISCOVERED ☐ CONNECTED ☐ TOOK ACTION

OUR ACTIVITIES WERE...
☐ GIRL-LED ☐ HANDS-ON ☐ COOPERATIVE

ATTENDANCE:
LOW ○ ○ ○ ○ ○ HIGH

ENJOYMENT:
LOW ○ ○ ○ ○ ○ HIGH

ENGAGEMENT:
LOW ○ ○ ○ ○ ○ HIGH

WHAT WAS MOST SUCCESSFUL?

WHAT COULD IMPROVE?

MEETING PLANNER

DATE:

MEETING DETAILS

TIME: .... LOCATION: .... BADGE/JOURNEY/AWARD: ....

MEETING GOAL/THEME: ....

PRE-MEETING PREP:

SUPPLIES:
- ☐
- ☐
- ☐
- ☐
- ☐

VOLUNTEERS:
- ☐
- ☐
- ☐
- ☐
- ☐

REMINDERS:

MEETING STRUCTURE:

START-UP ACTIVITY:

_____

OPENING:

_____

BUSINESS:

_____

ACTIVITIES:

(1)

(2)

(3)

(4)

(5)

_____

CLEAN-UP & CLOSING:

NEXT MEETING:

REFLECTION:

DURING THIS MEETING, THE GIRLS...
☐ DISCOVERED ☐ CONNECTED ☐ TOOK ACTION

OUR ACTIVITIES WERE...
☐ GIRL-LED ☐ HANDS-ON ☐ COOPERATIVE

ATTENDANCE:
LOW ○ ○ ○ ○ ○ HIGH

ENJOYMENT:
LOW ○ ○ ○ ○ ○ HIGH

ENGAGEMENT:
LOW ○ ○ ○ ○ ○ HIGH

WHAT WAS MOST SUCCESSFUL?

WHAT COULD IMPROVE?

MEETING PLANNER

DATE:

MEETING DETAILS

TIME: .... LOCATION: .... BADGE/JOURNEY/AWARD: ....

MEETING GOAL/THEME: ....

PRE-MEETING PREP:

SUPPLIES:
- ☐
- ☐
- ☐
- ☐
- ☐

VOLUNTEERS:
- ☐
- ☐
- ☐
- ☐
- ☐

REMINDERS:

MEETING STRUCTURE:

START-UP ACTIVITY:

___

OPENING:

___

BUSINESS:

___

ACTIVITIES:

(1)

(2)

(3)

(4)

(5)

___

CLEAN-UP & CLOSING:

NEXT MEETING:

REFLECTION:

DURING THIS MEETING, THE GIRLS...
☐ DISCOVERED ☐ CONNECTED ☐ TOOK ACTION

OUR ACTIVITIES WERE...
☐ GIRL-LED ☐ HANDS-ON ☐ COOPERATIVE

ATTENDANCE:
LOW ○ ○ ○ ○ ○ HIGH

ENJOYMENT:
LOW ○ ○ ○ ○ ○ HIGH

ENGAGEMENT:
LOW ○ ○ ○ ○ ○ HIGH

WHAT WAS MOST SUCCESSFUL?

WHAT COULD IMPROVE?

MEETING PLANNER

DATE:

MEETING DETAILS
TIME: .... LOCATION: .... BADGE/JOURNEY/AWARD: ....

MEETING GOAL/THEME: ....

PRE-MEETING PREP:

SUPPLIES:
- ☐
- ☐
- ☐
- ☐
- ☐

VOLUNTEERS:
- ☐
- ☐
- ☐
- ☐
- ☐

REMINDERS:

MEETING STRUCTURE:

START-UP ACTIVITY:

___

OPENING:

___

BUSINESS:

___

ACTIVITIES:

(1)

(2)

(3)

(4)

(5)

___

CLEAN-UP & CLOSING:

NEXT MEETING:

REFLECTION:

DURING THIS MEETING, THE GIRLS...
☐ DISCOVERED ☐ CONNECTED ☐ TOOK ACTION

OUR ACTIVITIES WERE...
☐ GIRL-LED ☐ HANDS-ON ☐ COOPERATIVE

ATTENDANCE:
LOW ○ ○ ○ ○ ○ HIGH

ENJOYMENT:
LOW ○ ○ ○ ○ ○ HIGH

ENGAGEMENT:
LOW ○ ○ ○ ○ ○ HIGH

WHAT WAS MOST SUCCESSFUL?

WHAT COULD IMPROVE?

MEETING PLANNER

DATE:

MEETING DETAILS

TIME: .... LOCATION: .... BADGE/JOURNEY/AWARD: ....

MEETING GOAL/THEME: ....

PRE-MEETING PREP:

SUPPLIES:
- ☐
- ☐
- ☐
- ☐
- ☐

VOLUNTEERS:
- ☐
- ☐
- ☐
- ☐
- ☐

REMINDERS:

MEETING STRUCTURE:

START-UP ACTIVITY:

_____

OPENING:

_____

BUSINESS:

_____

_____

ACTIVITIES:

(1)

(2)

(3)

(4)

(5)

_____

CLEAN-UP & CLOSING:

NEXT MEETING:

REFLECTION:

DURING THIS MEETING, THE GIRLS...
☐ DISCOVERED ☐ CONNECTED ☐ TOOK ACTION

OUR ACTIVITIES WERE...
☐ GIRL-LED ☐ HANDS-ON ☐ COOPERATIVE

ATTENDANCE:
LOW ○ ○ ○ ○ ○ HIGH

ENJOYMENT:
LOW ○ ○ ○ ○ ○ HIGH

ENGAGEMENT:
LOW ○ ○ ○ ○ ○ HIGH

WHAT WAS MOST SUCCESSFUL?

WHAT COULD IMPROVE?

MEETING PLANNER

DATE:

MEETING DETAILS
TIME: .... LOCATION: .... BADGE/JOURNEY/AWARD: ....

MEETING GOAL/THEME: ....

PRE-MEETING PREP:

SUPPLIES:
- ☐
- ☐
- ☐
- ☐
- ☐

VOLUNTEERS:
- ☐
- ☐
- ☐
- ☐
- ☐

REMINDERS:

MEETING STRUCTURE:

START-UP ACTIVITY:

OPENING:

BUSINESS:

ACTIVITIES:

(1)

(2)

(3)

(4)

(5)

CLEAN-UP & CLOSING:

NEXT MEETING:

REFLECTION:

DURING THIS MEETING, THE GIRLS...
☐ DISCOVERED ☐ CONNECTED ☐ TOOK ACTION

OUR ACTIVITIES WERE...
☐ GIRL-LED ☐ HANDS-ON ☐ COOPERATIVE

ATTENDANCE:
LOW ○ ○ ○ ○ ○ HIGH

ENJOYMENT:
LOW ○ ○ ○ ○ ○ HIGH

ENGAGEMENT:
LOW ○ ○ ○ ○ ○ HIGH

WHAT WAS MOST SUCCESSFUL?

WHAT COULD IMPROVE?

MEETING PLANNER

DATE:

MEETING DETAILS

TIME: .... LOCATION: .... BADGE/JOURNEY/AWARD: ....

MEETING GOAL/THEME: ....

PRE-MEETING PREP:

SUPPLIES:
- ☐
- ☐
- ☐
- ☐
- ☐

VOLUNTEERS:
- ☐
- ☐
- ☐
- ☐
- ☐

REMINDERS:

MEETING STRUCTURE:

START-UP ACTIVITY:

_____

OPENING:

_____

BUSINESS:

_____

ACTIVITIES:

(1)

(2)

(3)

(4)

(5)

_____

CLEAN-UP & CLOSING:

NEXT MEETING:

REFLECTION:

DURING THIS MEETING, THE GIRLS...
☐ DISCOVERED ☐ CONNECTED ☐ TOOK ACTION

OUR ACTIVITIES WERE...
☐ GIRL-LED ☐ HANDS-ON ☐ COOPERATIVE

ATTENDANCE:
LOW ○ ○ ○ ○ ○ HIGH

ENJOYMENT:
LOW ○ ○ ○ ○ ○ HIGH

ENGAGEMENT:
LOW ○ ○ ○ ○ ○ HIGH

WHAT WAS MOST SUCCESSFUL?

WHAT COULD IMPROVE?

MEETING PLANNER

DATE:

MEETING DETAILS
TIME: .... LOCATION: .... BADGE/JOURNEY/AWARD: ....

MEETING GOAL/THEME: ....

PRE-MEETING PREP:
SUPPLIES:
- ☐
- ☐
- ☐
- ☐
- ☐

VOLUNTEERS:
- ☐
- ☐
- ☐
- ☐
- ☐

REMINDERS:

MEETING STRUCTURE:
START-UP ACTIVITY:

___

OPENING:

___

BUSINESS:

___

ACTIVITIES:

(1)

(2)

(3)

(4)

(5)

___

CLEAN-UP & CLOSING:

NEXT MEETING:

REFLECTION:
DURING THIS MEETING, THE GIRLS...
☐ DISCOVERED ☐ CONNECTED ☐ TOOK ACTION

OUR ACTIVITIES WERE...
☐ GIRL-LED ☐ HANDS-ON ☐ COOPERATIVE

ATTENDANCE:
LOW ○ ○ ○ ○ ○ HIGH

ENJOYMENT:
LOW ○ ○ ○ ○ ○ HIGH

ENGAGEMENT:
LOW ○ ○ ○ ○ ○ HIGH

WHAT WAS MOST SUCCESSFUL?

WHAT COULD IMPROVE?

MEETING PLANNER

DATE:

MEETING DETAILS

TIME: .... LOCATION: .... BADGE/JOURNEY/AWARD: ....

MEETING GOAL/THEME: ....

PRE-MEETING PREP:

SUPPLIES:
- ☐
- ☐
- ☐
- ☐
- ☐

VOLUNTEERS:
- ☐
- ☐
- ☐
- ☐
- ☐

REMINDERS:

MEETING STRUCTURE:

START-UP ACTIVITY:

_____

OPENING:

_____

BUSINESS:

_____

ACTIVITIES:

(1)

(2)

(3)

(4)

(5)

_____

CLEAN-UP & CLOSING:

NEXT MEETING:

REFLECTION:

DURING THIS MEETING, THE GIRLS...
☐ DISCOVERED ☐ CONNECTED ☐ TOOK ACTION

OUR ACTIVITIES WERE...
☐ GIRL-LED ☐ HANDS-ON ☐ COOPERATIVE

ATTENDANCE:
LOW ○ ○ ○ ○ ○ HIGH

ENJOYMENT:
LOW ○ ○ ○ ○ ○ HIGH

ENGAGEMENT:
LOW ○ ○ ○ ○ ○ HIGH

WHAT WAS MOST SUCCESSFUL?

WHAT COULD IMPROVE?

MEETING PLANNER

DATE:

MEETING DETAILS
TIME: .... LOCATION: .... BADGE/JOURNEY/AWARD: ....

MEETING GOAL/THEME: ....

PRE-MEETING PREP:

SUPPLIES:
- ☐
- ☐
- ☐
- ☐
- ☐

VOLUNTEERS:
- ☐
- ☐
- ☐
- ☐
- ☐

REMINDERS:

MEETING STRUCTURE:

START-UP ACTIVITY:
_____

OPENING:
_____

BUSINESS:
_____
_____

ACTIVITIES:

(1)

(2)

(3)

(4)

(5)
_____

CLEAN-UP & CLOSING:

NEXT MEETING:

REFLECTION:

DURING THIS MEETING, THE GIRLS...
☐ DISCOVERED ☐ CONNECTED ☐ TOOK ACTION

OUR ACTIVITIES WERE...
☐ GIRL-LED ☐ HANDS-ON ☐ COOPERATIVE

ATTENDANCE:
LOW ◯ ◯ ◯ ◯ ◯ HIGH

ENJOYMENT:
LOW ◯ ◯ ◯ ◯ ◯ HIGH

ENGAGEMENT:
LOW ◯ ◯ ◯ ◯ ◯ HIGH

WHAT WAS MOST SUCCESSFUL?

WHAT COULD IMPROVE?

MEETING PLANNER

DATE:

MEETING DETAILS
TIME: .... LOCATION: .... BADGE/JOURNEY/AWARD: ....

MEETING GOAL/THEME: ....

PRE-MEETING PREP:

SUPPLIES:
- ☐
- ☐
- ☐
- ☐
- ☐

VOLUNTEERS:
- ☐
- ☐
- ☐
- ☐
- ☐

REMINDERS:

MEETING STRUCTURE:

START-UP ACTIVITY:
_____

OPENING:
_____

BUSINESS:
_____

ACTIVITIES:

(1)

(2)

(3)

(4)

(5)
_____

CLEAN-UP & CLOSING:

NEXT MEETING:

REFLECTION:

DURING THIS MEETING, THE GIRLS...
☐ DISCOVERED ☐ CONNECTED ☐ TOOK ACTION

OUR ACTIVITIES WERE...
☐ GIRL-LED ☐ HANDS-ON ☐ COOPERATIVE

ATTENDANCE:
LOW ○ ○ ○ ○ ○ HIGH

ENJOYMENT:
LOW ○ ○ ○ ○ ○ HIGH

ENGAGEMENT:
LOW ○ ○ ○ ○ ○ HIGH

WHAT WAS MOST SUCCESSFUL?

WHAT COULD IMPROVE?

BADGE ACTIVITIES PLANNER

BADGE: ....

PURPOSE: ....

 # OF MEETINGS TO COMPLETE THIS BADGE: .... **JOURNEY CONNECTION(S):** .... ☐ STEP 1 ☐ STEP 2 ☐ STEP 3 ☐ STEP 4 ☐ STEP 5

LONG-TERM PLANNING:

FIELD TRIP/GUEST SPEAKER IDEAS:

STEP 1:   **TIME NEEDED:** .... **MINUTES**

ACTIVITY: .... **TO BE COMPLETED AT:** ☐ HOME ☐ MEETING ☐ EVENT ☐ FIELD TRIP

PREP/SUPPLIES NEEDED: **WHO'S RESPONSIBLE?**

(1) .... ☐ LEADER ☐ GIRL/VOLUNTEER: ....

(2) .... ☐ LEADER ☐ GIRL/VOLUNTEER: ....

(3) .... ☐ LEADER ☐ GIRL/VOLUNTEER: ....

(4) .... ☐ LEADER ☐ GIRL/VOLUNTEER: ....

(5) .... ☐ LEADER ☐ GIRL/VOLUNTEER: ....

ACTIVITY STEPS/NOTES:

LEADERSHIP KEYS: ☐ DISCOVER ☐ CONNECT ☐ TAKE ACTION   **PROCESSES:** ☐ GIRL-LED ☐ LEARNING BY DOING ☐ COOPERATIVE LEARNING

STEP 2:   **TIME NEEDED:** .... **MINUTES**

ACTIVITY: .... **TO BE COMPLETED AT:** ☐ HOME ☐ MEETING ☐ EVENT ☐ FIELD TRIP

PREP/SUPPLIES NEEDED: **WHO'S RESPONSIBLE?**

(1) .... ☐ LEADER ☐ GIRL/VOLUNTEER: ....

(2) .... ☐ LEADER ☐ GIRL/VOLUNTEER: ....

(3) .... ☐ LEADER ☐ GIRL/VOLUNTEER: ....

(4) .... ☐ LEADER ☐ GIRL/VOLUNTEER: ....

(5) .... ☐ LEADER ☐ GIRL/VOLUNTEER: ....

ACTIVITY STEPS/NOTES:

LEADERSHIP KEYS: ☐ DISCOVER ☐ CONNECT ☐ TAKE ACTION   **PROCESSES:** ☐ GIRL-LED ☐ LEARNING BY DOING ☐ COOPERATIVE LEARNING

STEP 3:   TIME NEEDED: .... MINUTES

ACTIVITY: .... TO BE COMPLETED AT: ☐ HOME ☐ MEETING ☐ EVENT ☐ FIELD TRIP

PREP/SUPPLIES NEEDED: WHO'S RESPONSIBLE?

(1) .... ☐ LEADER ☐ GIRL/VOLUNTEER: ....

(2) .... ☐ LEADER ☐ GIRL/VOLUNTEER: ....

(3) .... ☐ LEADER ☐ GIRL/VOLUNTEER: ....

(4) .... ☐ LEADER ☐ GIRL/VOLUNTEER: ....

(5) .... ☐ LEADER ☐ GIRL/VOLUNTEER: ....

ACTIVITY STEPS/NOTES:

LEADERSHIP KEYS: ☐ DISCOVER ☐ CONNECT ☐ TAKE ACTION   PROCESSES: ☐ GIRL-LED ☐ LEARNING BY DOING ☐ COOPERATIVE LEARNING

STEP 4:   TIME NEEDED: .... MINUTES

ACTIVITY: .... TO BE COMPLETED AT: ☐ HOME ☐ MEETING ☐ EVENT ☐ FIELD TRIP

PREP/SUPPLIES NEEDED: WHO'S RESPONSIBLE?

(1) .... ☐ LEADER ☐ GIRL/VOLUNTEER: ....

(2) .... ☐ LEADER ☐ GIRL/VOLUNTEER: ....

(3) .... ☐ LEADER ☐ GIRL/VOLUNTEER: ....

(4) .... ☐ LEADER ☐ GIRL/VOLUNTEER: ....

(5) .... ☐ LEADER ☐ GIRL/VOLUNTEER: ....

ACTIVITY STEPS/NOTES:

LEADERSHIP KEYS: ☐ DISCOVER ☐ CONNECT ☐ TAKE ACTION   PROCESSES: ☐ GIRL-LED ☐ LEARNING BY DOING ☐ COOPERATIVE LEARNING

STEP 5:   TIME NEEDED: .... MINUTES

ACTIVITY: .... TO BE COMPLETED AT: ☐ HOME ☐ MEETING ☐ EVENT ☐ FIELD TRIP

PREP/SUPPLIES NEEDED: WHO'S RESPONSIBLE?

(1) .... ☐ LEADER ☐ GIRL/VOLUNTEER: ....

(2) .... ☐ LEADER ☐ GIRL/VOLUNTEER: ....

(3) .... ☐ LEADER ☐ GIRL/VOLUNTEER: ....

(4) .... ☐ LEADER ☐ GIRL/VOLUNTEER: ....

(5) .... ☐ LEADER ☐ GIRL/VOLUNTEER: ....

ACTIVITY STEPS/NOTES:

LEADERSHIP KEYS: ☐ DISCOVER ☐ CONNECT ☐ TAKE ACTION   PROCESSES: ☐ GIRL-LED ☐ LEARNING BY DOING ☐ COOPERATIVE LEARNING

BADGE ACTIVITIES PLANNER

BADGE: ....

PURPOSE: ....

 # OF MEETINGS TO COMPLETE THIS BADGE: .... **JOURNEY CONNECTION(S):** .... ☐ STEP 1 ☐ STEP 2 ☐ STEP 3 ☐ STEP 4 ☐ STEP 5

LONG-TERM PLANNING:

FIELD TRIP/GUEST SPEAKER IDEAS:

STEP 1: **TIME NEEDED:** .... MINUTES

ACTIVITY: .... **TO BE COMPLETED AT:** ☐ HOME ☐ MEETING ☐ EVENT ☐ FIELD TRIP

PREP/SUPPLIES NEEDED: **WHO'S RESPONSIBLE?**

(1) .... ☐ LEADER ☐ GIRL/VOLUNTEER: ....

(2) .... ☐ LEADER ☐ GIRL/VOLUNTEER: ....

(3) .... ☐ LEADER ☐ GIRL/VOLUNTEER: ....

(4) .... ☐ LEADER ☐ GIRL/VOLUNTEER: ....

(5) .... ☐ LEADER ☐ GIRL/VOLUNTEER: ....

ACTIVITY STEPS/NOTES:

LEADERSHIP KEYS: ☐ DISCOVER ☐ CONNECT ☐ TAKE ACTION   **PROCESSES:** ☐ GIRL-LED ☐ LEARNING BY DOING ☐ COOPERATIVE LEARNING

STEP 2: **TIME NEEDED:** .... MINUTES

ACTIVITY: .... **TO BE COMPLETED AT:** ☐ HOME ☐ MEETING ☐ EVENT ☐ FIELD TRIP

PREP/SUPPLIES NEEDED: **WHO'S RESPONSIBLE?**

(1) .... ☐ LEADER ☐ GIRL/VOLUNTEER: ....

(2) .... ☐ LEADER ☐ GIRL/VOLUNTEER: ....

(3) .... ☐ LEADER ☐ GIRL/VOLUNTEER: ....

(4) .... ☐ LEADER ☐ GIRL/VOLUNTEER: ....

(5) .... ☐ LEADER ☐ GIRL/VOLUNTEER: ....

ACTIVITY STEPS/NOTES:

LEADERSHIP KEYS: ☐ DISCOVER ☐ CONNECT ☐ TAKE ACTION   **PROCESSES:** ☐ GIRL-LED ☐ LEARNING BY DOING ☐ COOPERATIVE LEARNING

STEP 3: TIME NEEDED: .... MINUTES

ACTIVITY: .... TO BE COMPLETED AT: ☐ HOME ☐ MEETING ☐ EVENT ☐ FIELD TRIP

PREP/SUPPLIES NEEDED: WHO'S RESPONSIBLE?

(1) .... ☐ LEADER ☐ GIRL/VOLUNTEER: ....

(2) .... ☐ LEADER ☐ GIRL/VOLUNTEER: ....

(3) .... ☐ LEADER ☐ GIRL/VOLUNTEER: ....

(4) .... ☐ LEADER ☐ GIRL/VOLUNTEER: ....

(5) .... ☐ LEADER ☐ GIRL/VOLUNTEER: ....

ACTIVITY STEPS/NOTES:

LEADERSHIP KEYS: ☐ DISCOVER ☐ CONNECT ☐ TAKE ACTION   PROCESSES: ☐ GIRL-LED ☐ LEARNING BY DOING ☐ COOPERATIVE LEARNING

STEP 4: TIME NEEDED: .... MINUTES

ACTIVITY: .... TO BE COMPLETED AT: ☐ HOME ☐ MEETING ☐ EVENT ☐ FIELD TRIP

PREP/SUPPLIES NEEDED: WHO'S RESPONSIBLE?

(1) .... ☐ LEADER ☐ GIRL/VOLUNTEER: ....

(2) .... ☐ LEADER ☐ GIRL/VOLUNTEER: ....

(3) .... ☐ LEADER ☐ GIRL/VOLUNTEER: ....

(4) .... ☐ LEADER ☐ GIRL/VOLUNTEER: ....

(5) .... ☐ LEADER ☐ GIRL/VOLUNTEER: ....

ACTIVITY STEPS/NOTES:

LEADERSHIP KEYS: ☐ DISCOVER ☐ CONNECT ☐ TAKE ACTION   PROCESSES: ☐ GIRL-LED ☐ LEARNING BY DOING ☐ COOPERATIVE LEARNING

STEP 5: TIME NEEDED: .... MINUTES

ACTIVITY: .... TO BE COMPLETED AT: ☐ HOME ☐ MEETING ☐ EVENT ☐ FIELD TRIP

PREP/SUPPLIES NEEDED: WHO'S RESPONSIBLE?

(1) .... ☐ LEADER ☐ GIRL/VOLUNTEER: ....

(2) .... ☐ LEADER ☐ GIRL/VOLUNTEER: ....

(3) .... ☐ LEADER ☐ GIRL/VOLUNTEER: ....

(4) .... ☐ LEADER ☐ GIRL/VOLUNTEER: ....

(5) .... ☐ LEADER ☐ GIRL/VOLUNTEER: ....

ACTIVITY STEPS/NOTES:

LEADERSHIP KEYS: ☐ DISCOVER ☐ CONNECT ☐ TAKE ACTION   PROCESSES: ☐ GIRL-LED ☐ LEARNING BY DOING ☐ COOPERATIVE LEARNING

BADGE ACTIVITIES PLANNER

BADGE: ....
PURPOSE: ....

OF MEETINGS TO COMPLETE THIS BADGE: .... JOURNEY CONNECTION(S): .... ☐ STEP 1 ☐ STEP 2 ☐ STEP 3 ☐ STEP 4 ☐ STEP 5

LONG-TERM PLANNING:

FIELD TRIP/GUEST SPEAKER IDEAS:

STEP 1: .... TIME NEEDED: .... MINUTES

ACTIVITY: .... TO BE COMPLETED AT: ☐ HOME ☐ MEETING ☐ EVENT ☐ FIELD TRIP

PREP/SUPPLIES NEEDED: WHO'S RESPONSIBLE?

(1) ....   ☐ LEADER ☐ GIRL/VOLUNTEER: ....
(2) ....   ☐ LEADER ☐ GIRL/VOLUNTEER: ....
(3) ....   ☐ LEADER ☐ GIRL/VOLUNTEER: ....
(4) ....   ☐ LEADER ☐ GIRL/VOLUNTEER: ....
(5) ....   ☐ LEADER ☐ GIRL/VOLUNTEER: ....

ACTIVITY STEPS/NOTES:

LEADERSHIP KEYS: ☐ DISCOVER ☐ CONNECT ☐ TAKE ACTION   PROCESSES: ☐ GIRL-LED ☐ LEARNING BY DOING ☐ COOPERATIVE LEARNING

STEP 2: .... TIME NEEDED: .... MINUTES

ACTIVITY: .... TO BE COMPLETED AT: ☐ HOME ☐ MEETING ☐ EVENT ☐ FIELD TRIP

PREP/SUPPLIES NEEDED: WHO'S RESPONSIBLE?

(1) ....   ☐ LEADER ☐ GIRL/VOLUNTEER: ....
(2) ....   ☐ LEADER ☐ GIRL/VOLUNTEER: ....
(3) ....   ☐ LEADER ☐ GIRL/VOLUNTEER: ....
(4) ....   ☐ LEADER ☐ GIRL/VOLUNTEER: ....
(5) ....   ☐ LEADER ☐ GIRL/VOLUNTEER: ....

ACTIVITY STEPS/NOTES:

LEADERSHIP KEYS: ☐ DISCOVER ☐ CONNECT ☐ TAKE ACTION   PROCESSES: ☐ GIRL-LED ☐ LEARNING BY DOING ☐ COOPERATIVE LEARNING

STEP 3:

TIME NEEDED: .... MINUTES

ACTIVITY: .... TO BE COMPLETED AT: ☐ HOME ☐ MEETING ☐ EVENT ☐ FIELD TRIP

PREP/SUPPLIES NEEDED:

WHO'S RESPONSIBLE?

(1) .... ☐ LEADER ☐ GIRL/VOLUNTEER: ....
(2) .... ☐ LEADER ☐ GIRL/VOLUNTEER: ....
(3) .... ☐ LEADER ☐ GIRL/VOLUNTEER: ....
(4) .... ☐ LEADER ☐ GIRL/VOLUNTEER: ....
(5) .... ☐ LEADER ☐ GIRL/VOLUNTEER: ....

ACTIVITY STEPS/NOTES:

LEADERSHIP KEYS: ☐ DISCOVER ☐ CONNECT ☐ TAKE ACTION   PROCESSES: ☐ GIRL-LED ☐ LEARNING BY DOING ☐ COOPERATIVE LEARNING

STEP 4:

TIME NEEDED: .... MINUTES

ACTIVITY: .... TO BE COMPLETED AT: ☐ HOME ☐ MEETING ☐ EVENT ☐ FIELD TRIP

PREP/SUPPLIES NEEDED:

WHO'S RESPONSIBLE?

(1) .... ☐ LEADER ☐ GIRL/VOLUNTEER: ....
(2) .... ☐ LEADER ☐ GIRL/VOLUNTEER: ....
(3) .... ☐ LEADER ☐ GIRL/VOLUNTEER: ....
(4) .... ☐ LEADER ☐ GIRL/VOLUNTEER: ....
(5) .... ☐ LEADER ☐ GIRL/VOLUNTEER: ....

ACTIVITY STEPS/NOTES:

LEADERSHIP KEYS: ☐ DISCOVER ☐ CONNECT ☐ TAKE ACTION   PROCESSES: ☐ GIRL-LED ☐ LEARNING BY DOING ☐ COOPERATIVE LEARNING

STEP 5:

TIME NEEDED: .... MINUTES

ACTIVITY: .... TO BE COMPLETED AT: ☐ HOME ☐ MEETING ☐ EVENT ☐ FIELD TRIP

PREP/SUPPLIES NEEDED:

WHO'S RESPONSIBLE?

(1) .... ☐ LEADER ☐ GIRL/VOLUNTEER: ....
(2) .... ☐ LEADER ☐ GIRL/VOLUNTEER: ....
(3) .... ☐ LEADER ☐ GIRL/VOLUNTEER: ....
(4) .... ☐ LEADER ☐ GIRL/VOLUNTEER: ....
(5) .... ☐ LEADER ☐ GIRL/VOLUNTEER: ....

ACTIVITY STEPS/NOTES:

LEADERSHIP KEYS: ☐ DISCOVER ☐ CONNECT ☐ TAKE ACTION   PROCESSES: ☐ GIRL-LED ☐ LEARNING BY DOING ☐ COOPERATIVE LEARNING

BADGE ACTIVITIES PLANNER

BADGE: ....

PURPOSE: ....

 # OF MEETINGS TO COMPLETE THIS BADGE: .... **JOURNEY CONNECTION(S):** .... ☐ STEP 1 ☐ STEP 2 ☐ STEP 3 ☐ STEP 4 ☐ STEP 5

LONG-TERM PLANNING:

FIELD TRIP/GUEST SPEAKER IDEAS:

STEP 1: .... **TIME NEEDED:** .... **MINUTES**

ACTIVITY: .... **TO BE COMPLETED AT:** ☐ HOME ☐ MEETING ☐ EVENT ☐ FIELD TRIP

PREP/SUPPLIES NEEDED: **WHO'S RESPONSIBLE?**

(1) .... ☐ LEADER ☐ GIRL/VOLUNTEER: ....

(2) .... ☐ LEADER ☐ GIRL/VOLUNTEER: ....

(3) .... ☐ LEADER ☐ GIRL/VOLUNTEER: ....

(4) .... ☐ LEADER ☐ GIRL/VOLUNTEER: ....

(5) .... ☐ LEADER ☐ GIRL/VOLUNTEER: ....

ACTIVITY STEPS/NOTES:

LEADERSHIP KEYS: ☐ DISCOVER ☐ CONNECT ☐ TAKE ACTION   **PROCESSES:** ☐ GIRL-LED ☐ LEARNING BY DOING ☐ COOPERATIVE LEARNING

STEP 2: .... **TIME NEEDED:** .... **MINUTES**

ACTIVITY: .... **TO BE COMPLETED AT:** ☐ HOME ☐ MEETING ☐ EVENT ☐ FIELD TRIP

PREP/SUPPLIES NEEDED: **WHO'S RESPONSIBLE?**

(1) .... ☐ LEADER ☐ GIRL/VOLUNTEER: ....

(2) .... ☐ LEADER ☐ GIRL/VOLUNTEER: ....

(3) .... ☐ LEADER ☐ GIRL/VOLUNTEER: ....

(4) .... ☐ LEADER ☐ GIRL/VOLUNTEER: ....

(5) .... ☐ LEADER ☐ GIRL/VOLUNTEER: ....

ACTIVITY STEPS/NOTES:

LEADERSHIP KEYS: ☐ DISCOVER ☐ CONNECT ☐ TAKE ACTION   **PROCESSES:** ☐ GIRL-LED ☐ LEARNING BY DOING ☐ COOPERATIVE LEARNING

STEP 3:

TIME NEEDED: .... MINUTES

ACTIVITY: .... TO BE COMPLETED AT: ☐ HOME ☐ MEETING ☐ EVENT ☐ FIELD TRIP

PREP/SUPPLIES NEEDED: WHO'S RESPONSIBLE?

(1) .... ☐ LEADER ☐ GIRL/VOLUNTEER: ....
(2) .... ☐ LEADER ☐ GIRL/VOLUNTEER: ....
(3) .... ☐ LEADER ☐ GIRL/VOLUNTEER: ....
(4) .... ☐ LEADER ☐ GIRL/VOLUNTEER: ....
(5) .... ☐ LEADER ☐ GIRL/VOLUNTEER: ....

ACTIVITY STEPS/NOTES:

LEADERSHIP KEYS: ☐ DISCOVER ☐ CONNECT ☐ TAKE ACTION   PROCESSES: ☐ GIRL-LED ☐ LEARNING BY DOING ☐ COOPERATIVE LEARNING

STEP 4:

TIME NEEDED: .... MINUTES

ACTIVITY: .... TO BE COMPLETED AT: ☐ HOME ☐ MEETING ☐ EVENT ☐ FIELD TRIP

PREP/SUPPLIES NEEDED: WHO'S RESPONSIBLE?

(1) .... ☐ LEADER ☐ GIRL/VOLUNTEER: ....
(2) .... ☐ LEADER ☐ GIRL/VOLUNTEER: ....
(3) .... ☐ LEADER ☐ GIRL/VOLUNTEER: ....
(4) .... ☐ LEADER ☐ GIRL/VOLUNTEER: ....
(5) .... ☐ LEADER ☐ GIRL/VOLUNTEER: ....

ACTIVITY STEPS/NOTES:

LEADERSHIP KEYS: ☐ DISCOVER ☐ CONNECT ☐ TAKE ACTION   PROCESSES: ☐ GIRL-LED ☐ LEARNING BY DOING ☐ COOPERATIVE LEARNING

STEP 5:

TIME NEEDED: .... MINUTES

ACTIVITY: .... TO BE COMPLETED AT: ☐ HOME ☐ MEETING ☐ EVENT ☐ FIELD TRIP

PREP/SUPPLIES NEEDED: WHO'S RESPONSIBLE?

(1) .... ☐ LEADER ☐ GIRL/VOLUNTEER: ....
(2) .... ☐ LEADER ☐ GIRL/VOLUNTEER: ....
(3) .... ☐ LEADER ☐ GIRL/VOLUNTEER: ....
(4) .... ☐ LEADER ☐ GIRL/VOLUNTEER: ....
(5) .... ☐ LEADER ☐ GIRL/VOLUNTEER: ....

ACTIVITY STEPS/NOTES:

LEADERSHIP KEYS: ☐ DISCOVER ☐ CONNECT ☐ TAKE ACTION   PROCESSES: ☐ GIRL-LED ☐ LEARNING BY DOING ☐ COOPERATIVE LEARNING

BADGE ACTIVITIES PLANNER

BADGE: ....

PURPOSE: ....

OF MEETINGS TO COMPLETE THIS BADGE: .... JOURNEY CONNECTION(S): .... ☐ STEP 1 ☐ STEP 2 ☐ STEP 3 ☐ STEP 4 ☐ STEP 5

LONG-TERM PLANNING:

FIELD TRIP/GUEST SPEAKER IDEAS:

STEP 1: .... TIME NEEDED: .... MINUTES

ACTIVITY: .... TO BE COMPLETED AT: ☐ HOME ☐ MEETING ☐ EVENT ☐ FIELD TRIP

PREP/SUPPLIES NEEDED: WHO'S RESPONSIBLE?

(1) .... ☐ LEADER ☐ GIRL/VOLUNTEER: ....

(2) .... ☐ LEADER ☐ GIRL/VOLUNTEER: ....

(3) .... ☐ LEADER ☐ GIRL/VOLUNTEER: ....

(4) .... ☐ LEADER ☐ GIRL/VOLUNTEER: ....

(5) .... ☐ LEADER ☐ GIRL/VOLUNTEER: ....

ACTIVITY STEPS/NOTES:

LEADERSHIP KEYS: ☐ DISCOVER ☐ CONNECT ☐ TAKE ACTION   PROCESSES: ☐ GIRL-LED ☐ LEARNING BY DOING ☐ COOPERATIVE LEARNING

STEP 2: .... TIME NEEDED: .... MINUTES

ACTIVITY: .... TO BE COMPLETED AT: ☐ HOME ☐ MEETING ☐ EVENT ☐ FIELD TRIP

PREP/SUPPLIES NEEDED: WHO'S RESPONSIBLE?

(1) .... ☐ LEADER ☐ GIRL/VOLUNTEER: ....

(2) .... ☐ LEADER ☐ GIRL/VOLUNTEER: ....

(3) .... ☐ LEADER ☐ GIRL/VOLUNTEER: ....

(4) .... ☐ LEADER ☐ GIRL/VOLUNTEER: ....

(5) .... ☐ LEADER ☐ GIRL/VOLUNTEER: ....

ACTIVITY STEPS/NOTES:

LEADERSHIP KEYS: ☐ DISCOVER ☐ CONNECT ☐ TAKE ACTION   PROCESSES: ☐ GIRL-LED ☐ LEARNING BY DOING ☐ COOPERATIVE LEARNING

STEP 3:

TIME NEEDED: .... MINUTES

ACTIVITY: .... TO BE COMPLETED AT: ☐ HOME ☐ MEETING ☐ EVENT ☐ FIELD TRIP

PREP/SUPPLIES NEEDED: WHO'S RESPONSIBLE?

(1) .... ☐ LEADER ☐ GIRL/VOLUNTEER: ....

(2) .... ☐ LEADER ☐ GIRL/VOLUNTEER: ....

(3) .... ☐ LEADER ☐ GIRL/VOLUNTEER: ....

(4) .... ☐ LEADER ☐ GIRL/VOLUNTEER: ....

(5) .... ☐ LEADER ☐ GIRL/VOLUNTEER: ....

ACTIVITY STEPS/NOTES:

LEADERSHIP KEYS: ☐ DISCOVER ☐ CONNECT ☐ TAKE ACTION   PROCESSES: ☐ GIRL-LED ☐ LEARNING BY DOING ☐ COOPERATIVE LEARNING

STEP 4:

TIME NEEDED: .... MINUTES

ACTIVITY: .... TO BE COMPLETED AT: ☐ HOME ☐ MEETING ☐ EVENT ☐ FIELD TRIP

PREP/SUPPLIES NEEDED: WHO'S RESPONSIBLE?

(1) .... ☐ LEADER ☐ GIRL/VOLUNTEER: ....

(2) .... ☐ LEADER ☐ GIRL/VOLUNTEER: ....

(3) .... ☐ LEADER ☐ GIRL/VOLUNTEER: ....

(4) .... ☐ LEADER ☐ GIRL/VOLUNTEER: ....

(5) .... ☐ LEADER ☐ GIRL/VOLUNTEER: ....

ACTIVITY STEPS/NOTES:

LEADERSHIP KEYS: ☐ DISCOVER ☐ CONNECT ☐ TAKE ACTION   PROCESSES: ☐ GIRL-LED ☐ LEARNING BY DOING ☐ COOPERATIVE LEARNING

STEP 5:

TIME NEEDED: .... MINUTES

ACTIVITY: .... TO BE COMPLETED AT: ☐ HOME ☐ MEETING ☐ EVENT ☐ FIELD TRIP

PREP/SUPPLIES NEEDED: WHO'S RESPONSIBLE?

(1) .... ☐ LEADER ☐ GIRL/VOLUNTEER: ....

(2) .... ☐ LEADER ☐ GIRL/VOLUNTEER: ....

(3) .... ☐ LEADER ☐ GIRL/VOLUNTEER: ....

(4) .... ☐ LEADER ☐ GIRL/VOLUNTEER: ....

(5) .... ☐ LEADER ☐ GIRL/VOLUNTEER: ....

ACTIVITY STEPS/NOTES:

LEADERSHIP KEYS: ☐ DISCOVER ☐ CONNECT ☐ TAKE ACTION   PROCESSES: ☐ GIRL-LED ☐ LEARNING BY DOING ☐ COOPERATIVE LEARNING

BADGE ACTIVITIES PLANNER

BADGE: ....

PURPOSE: ....

 # OF MEETINGS TO COMPLETE THIS BADGE: .... **JOURNEY CONNECTION(S):** .... ☐ STEP 1 ☐ STEP 2 ☐ STEP 3 ☐ STEP 4 ☐ STEP 5

LONG-TERM PLANNING:

FIELD TRIP/GUEST SPEAKER IDEAS:

STEP 1:   **TIME NEEDED:** .... **MINUTES**

ACTIVITY: .... **TO BE COMPLETED AT:** ☐ HOME ☐ MEETING ☐ EVENT ☐ FIELD TRIP

PREP/SUPPLIES NEEDED: **WHO'S RESPONSIBLE?**

(1) .... ☐ LEADER ☐ GIRL/VOLUNTEER: ....

(2) .... ☐ LEADER ☐ GIRL/VOLUNTEER: ....

(3) .... ☐ LEADER ☐ GIRL/VOLUNTEER: ....

(4) .... ☐ LEADER ☐ GIRL/VOLUNTEER: ....

(5) .... ☐ LEADER ☐ GIRL/VOLUNTEER: ....

ACTIVITY STEPS/NOTES:

LEADERSHIP KEYS: ☐ DISCOVER ☐ CONNECT ☐ TAKE ACTION   **PROCESSES:** ☐ GIRL-LED ☐ LEARNING BY DOING ☐ COOPERATIVE LEARNING

STEP 2:   **TIME NEEDED:** .... **MINUTES**

ACTIVITY: .... **TO BE COMPLETED AT:** ☐ HOME ☐ MEETING ☐ EVENT ☐ FIELD TRIP

PREP/SUPPLIES NEEDED: **WHO'S RESPONSIBLE?**

(1) .... ☐ LEADER ☐ GIRL/VOLUNTEER: ....

(2) .... ☐ LEADER ☐ GIRL/VOLUNTEER: ....

(3) .... ☐ LEADER ☐ GIRL/VOLUNTEER: ....

(4) .... ☐ LEADER ☐ GIRL/VOLUNTEER: ....

(5) .... ☐ LEADER ☐ GIRL/VOLUNTEER: ....

ACTIVITY STEPS/NOTES:

LEADERSHIP KEYS: ☐ DISCOVER ☐ CONNECT ☐ TAKE ACTION   **PROCESSES:** ☐ GIRL-LED ☐ LEARNING BY DOING ☐ COOPERATIVE LEARNING

STEP 3:

TIME NEEDED: .... MINUTES

ACTIVITY: .... TO BE COMPLETED AT: ☐ HOME ☐ MEETING ☐ EVENT ☐ FIELD TRIP

PREP/SUPPLIES NEEDED: WHO'S RESPONSIBLE?

(1) .... ☐ LEADER ☐ GIRL/VOLUNTEER: ....

(2) .... ☐ LEADER ☐ GIRL/VOLUNTEER: ....

(3) .... ☐ LEADER ☐ GIRL/VOLUNTEER: ....

(4) .... ☐ LEADER ☐ GIRL/VOLUNTEER: ....

(5) .... ☐ LEADER ☐ GIRL/VOLUNTEER: ....

ACTIVITY STEPS/NOTES:

LEADERSHIP KEYS: ☐ DISCOVER ☐ CONNECT ☐ TAKE ACTION   PROCESSES: ☐ GIRL-LED ☐ LEARNING BY DOING ☐ COOPERATIVE LEARNING

STEP 4:

TIME NEEDED: .... MINUTES

ACTIVITY: .... TO BE COMPLETED AT: ☐ HOME ☐ MEETING ☐ EVENT ☐ FIELD TRIP

PREP/SUPPLIES NEEDED: WHO'S RESPONSIBLE?

(1) .... ☐ LEADER ☐ GIRL/VOLUNTEER: ....

(2) .... ☐ LEADER ☐ GIRL/VOLUNTEER: ....

(3) .... ☐ LEADER ☐ GIRL/VOLUNTEER: ....

(4) .... ☐ LEADER ☐ GIRL/VOLUNTEER: ....

(5) .... ☐ LEADER ☐ GIRL/VOLUNTEER: ....

ACTIVITY STEPS/NOTES:

LEADERSHIP KEYS: ☐ DISCOVER ☐ CONNECT ☐ TAKE ACTION   PROCESSES: ☐ GIRL-LED ☐ LEARNING BY DOING ☐ COOPERATIVE LEARNING

STEP 5:

TIME NEEDED: .... MINUTES

ACTIVITY: .... TO BE COMPLETED AT: ☐ HOME ☐ MEETING ☐ EVENT ☐ FIELD TRIP

PREP/SUPPLIES NEEDED: WHO'S RESPONSIBLE?

(1) .... ☐ LEADER ☐ GIRL/VOLUNTEER: ....

(2) .... ☐ LEADER ☐ GIRL/VOLUNTEER: ....

(3) .... ☐ LEADER ☐ GIRL/VOLUNTEER: ....

(4) .... ☐ LEADER ☐ GIRL/VOLUNTEER: ....

(5) .... ☐ LEADER ☐ GIRL/VOLUNTEER: ....

ACTIVITY STEPS/NOTES:

LEADERSHIP KEYS: ☐ DISCOVER ☐ CONNECT ☐ TAKE ACTION   PROCESSES: ☐ GIRL-LED ☐ LEARNING BY DOING ☐ COOPERATIVE LEARNING

BADGE ACTIVITIES PLANNER

BADGE: ....

PURPOSE: ....

 # OF MEETINGS TO COMPLETE THIS BADGE: .... **JOURNEY CONNECTION(S):** .... ☐ STEP 1 ☐ STEP 2 ☐ STEP 3 ☐ STEP 4 ☐ STEP 5

LONG-TERM PLANNING:

FIELD TRIP/GUEST SPEAKER IDEAS:

STEP 1:   **TIME NEEDED:** .... MINUTES

ACTIVITY: .... **TO BE COMPLETED AT:** ☐ HOME ☐ MEETING ☐ EVENT ☐ FIELD TRIP

PREP/SUPPLIES NEEDED: **WHO'S RESPONSIBLE?**

(1) .... ☐ LEADER ☐ GIRL/VOLUNTEER: ....

(2) .... ☐ LEADER ☐ GIRL/VOLUNTEER: ....

(3) .... ☐ LEADER ☐ GIRL/VOLUNTEER: ....

(4) .... ☐ LEADER ☐ GIRL/VOLUNTEER: ....

(5) .... ☐ LEADER ☐ GIRL/VOLUNTEER: ....

ACTIVITY STEPS/NOTES:

LEADERSHIP KEYS: ☐ DISCOVER ☐ CONNECT ☐ TAKE ACTION   **PROCESSES:** ☐ GIRL-LED ☐ LEARNING BY DOING ☐ COOPERATIVE LEARNING

STEP 2:   **TIME NEEDED:** .... MINUTES

ACTIVITY: .... **TO BE COMPLETED AT:** ☐ HOME ☐ MEETING ☐ EVENT ☐ FIELD TRIP

PREP/SUPPLIES NEEDED: **WHO'S RESPONSIBLE?**

(1) .... ☐ LEADER ☐ GIRL/VOLUNTEER: ....

(2) .... ☐ LEADER ☐ GIRL/VOLUNTEER: ....

(3) .... ☐ LEADER ☐ GIRL/VOLUNTEER: ....

(4) .... ☐ LEADER ☐ GIRL/VOLUNTEER: ....

(5) .... ☐ LEADER ☐ GIRL/VOLUNTEER: ....

ACTIVITY STEPS/NOTES:

LEADERSHIP KEYS: ☐ DISCOVER ☐ CONNECT ☐ TAKE ACTION   **PROCESSES:** ☐ GIRL-LED ☐ LEARNING BY DOING ☐ COOPERATIVE LEARNING

STEP 3:   TIME NEEDED: .... MINUTES

ACTIVITY: .... TO BE COMPLETED AT: ☐ HOME ☐ MEETING ☐ EVENT ☐ FIELD TRIP

PREP/SUPPLIES NEEDED: WHO'S RESPONSIBLE?

(1) .... ☐ LEADER ☐ GIRL/VOLUNTEER: ....

(2) .... ☐ LEADER ☐ GIRL/VOLUNTEER: ....

(3) .... ☐ LEADER ☐ GIRL/VOLUNTEER: ....

(4) .... ☐ LEADER ☐ GIRL/VOLUNTEER: ....

(5) .... ☐ LEADER ☐ GIRL/VOLUNTEER: ....

ACTIVITY STEPS/NOTES:

LEADERSHIP KEYS: ☐ DISCOVER ☐ CONNECT ☐ TAKE ACTION   PROCESSES: ☐ GIRL-LED ☐ LEARNING BY DOING ☐ COOPERATIVE LEARNING

STEP 4:   TIME NEEDED: .... MINUTES

ACTIVITY: .... TO BE COMPLETED AT: ☐ HOME ☐ MEETING ☐ EVENT ☐ FIELD TRIP

PREP/SUPPLIES NEEDED: WHO'S RESPONSIBLE?

(1) .... ☐ LEADER ☐ GIRL/VOLUNTEER: ....

(2) .... ☐ LEADER ☐ GIRL/VOLUNTEER: ....

(3) .... ☐ LEADER ☐ GIRL/VOLUNTEER: ....

(4) .... ☐ LEADER ☐ GIRL/VOLUNTEER: ....

(5) .... ☐ LEADER ☐ GIRL/VOLUNTEER: ....

ACTIVITY STEPS/NOTES:

LEADERSHIP KEYS: ☐ DISCOVER ☐ CONNECT ☐ TAKE ACTION   PROCESSES: ☐ GIRL-LED ☐ LEARNING BY DOING ☐ COOPERATIVE LEARNING

STEP 5:   TIME NEEDED: .... MINUTES

ACTIVITY: .... TO BE COMPLETED AT: ☐ HOME ☐ MEETING ☐ EVENT ☐ FIELD TRIP

PREP/SUPPLIES NEEDED: WHO'S RESPONSIBLE?

(1) .... ☐ LEADER ☐ GIRL/VOLUNTEER: ....

(2) .... ☐ LEADER ☐ GIRL/VOLUNTEER: ....

(3) .... ☐ LEADER ☐ GIRL/VOLUNTEER: ....

(4) .... ☐ LEADER ☐ GIRL/VOLUNTEER: ....

(5) .... ☐ LEADER ☐ GIRL/VOLUNTEER: ....

ACTIVITY STEPS/NOTES:

LEADERSHIP KEYS: ☐ DISCOVER ☐ CONNECT ☐ TAKE ACTION   PROCESSES: ☐ GIRL-LED ☐ LEARNING BY DOING ☐ COOPERATIVE LEARNING

BADGE ACTIVITIES PLANNER

BADGE: ....

PURPOSE: ....

 # OF MEETINGS TO COMPLETE THIS BADGE: .... **JOURNEY CONNECTION(S):** .... ☐ STEP 1 ☐ STEP 2 ☐ STEP 3 ☐ STEP 4 ☐ STEP 5

LONG-TERM PLANNING:

FIELD TRIP/GUEST SPEAKER IDEAS:

STEP 1:   **TIME NEEDED:** .... **MINUTES**

ACTIVITY: .... **TO BE COMPLETED AT:** ☐ HOME ☐ MEETING ☐ EVENT ☐ FIELD TRIP

PREP/SUPPLIES NEEDED: **WHO'S RESPONSIBLE?**

(1) .... ☐ LEADER ☐ GIRL/VOLUNTEER: ....

(2) .... ☐ LEADER ☐ GIRL/VOLUNTEER: ....

(3) .... ☐ LEADER ☐ GIRL/VOLUNTEER: ....

(4) .... ☐ LEADER ☐ GIRL/VOLUNTEER: ....

(5) .... ☐ LEADER ☐ GIRL/VOLUNTEER: ....

ACTIVITY STEPS/NOTES:

LEADERSHIP KEYS: ☐ DISCOVER ☐ CONNECT ☐ TAKE ACTION   **PROCESSES:** ☐ GIRL-LED ☐ LEARNING BY DOING ☐ COOPERATIVE LEARNING

STEP 2:   **TIME NEEDED:** .... **MINUTES**

ACTIVITY: .... **TO BE COMPLETED AT:** ☐ HOME ☐ MEETING ☐ EVENT ☐ FIELD TRIP

PREP/SUPPLIES NEEDED: **WHO'S RESPONSIBLE?**

(1) .... ☐ LEADER ☐ GIRL/VOLUNTEER: ....

(2) .... ☐ LEADER ☐ GIRL/VOLUNTEER: ....

(3) .... ☐ LEADER ☐ GIRL/VOLUNTEER: ....

(4) .... ☐ LEADER ☐ GIRL/VOLUNTEER: ....

(5) .... ☐ LEADER ☐ GIRL/VOLUNTEER: ....

ACTIVITY STEPS/NOTES:

LEADERSHIP KEYS: ☐ DISCOVER ☐ CONNECT ☐ TAKE ACTION   **PROCESSES:** ☐ GIRL-LED ☐ LEARNING BY DOING ☐ COOPERATIVE LEARNING

STEP 3:

TIME NEEDED: .... MINUTES

ACTIVITY: .... TO BE COMPLETED AT: ☐ HOME ☐ MEETING ☐ EVENT ☐ FIELD TRIP

PREP/SUPPLIES NEEDED: WHO'S RESPONSIBLE?

(1) .... ☐ LEADER ☐ GIRL/VOLUNTEER: ....
(2) .... ☐ LEADER ☐ GIRL/VOLUNTEER: ....
(3) .... ☐ LEADER ☐ GIRL/VOLUNTEER: ....
(4) .... ☐ LEADER ☐ GIRL/VOLUNTEER: ....
(5) .... ☐ LEADER ☐ GIRL/VOLUNTEER: ....

ACTIVITY STEPS/NOTES:

LEADERSHIP KEYS: ☐ DISCOVER ☐ CONNECT ☐ TAKE ACTION   PROCESSES: ☐ GIRL-LED ☐ LEARNING BY DOING ☐ COOPERATIVE LEARNING

STEP 4:

TIME NEEDED: .... MINUTES

ACTIVITY: .... TO BE COMPLETED AT: ☐ HOME ☐ MEETING ☐ EVENT ☐ FIELD TRIP

PREP/SUPPLIES NEEDED: WHO'S RESPONSIBLE?

(1) .... ☐ LEADER ☐ GIRL/VOLUNTEER: ....
(2) .... ☐ LEADER ☐ GIRL/VOLUNTEER: ....
(3) .... ☐ LEADER ☐ GIRL/VOLUNTEER: ....
(4) .... ☐ LEADER ☐ GIRL/VOLUNTEER: ....
(5) .... ☐ LEADER ☐ GIRL/VOLUNTEER: ....

ACTIVITY STEPS/NOTES:

LEADERSHIP KEYS: ☐ DISCOVER ☐ CONNECT ☐ TAKE ACTION   PROCESSES: ☐ GIRL-LED ☐ LEARNING BY DOING ☐ COOPERATIVE LEARNING

STEP 5:

TIME NEEDED: .... MINUTES

ACTIVITY: .... TO BE COMPLETED AT: ☐ HOME ☐ MEETING ☐ EVENT ☐ FIELD TRIP

PREP/SUPPLIES NEEDED: WHO'S RESPONSIBLE?

(1) .... ☐ LEADER ☐ GIRL/VOLUNTEER: ....
(2) .... ☐ LEADER ☐ GIRL/VOLUNTEER: ....
(3) .... ☐ LEADER ☐ GIRL/VOLUNTEER: ....
(4) .... ☐ LEADER ☐ GIRL/VOLUNTEER: ....
(5) .... ☐ LEADER ☐ GIRL/VOLUNTEER: ....

ACTIVITY STEPS/NOTES:

LEADERSHIP KEYS: ☐ DISCOVER ☐ CONNECT ☐ TAKE ACTION   PROCESSES: ☐ GIRL-LED ☐ LEARNING BY DOING ☐ COOPERATIVE LEARNING

BADGE ACTIVITIES PLANNER

BADGE: ....

PURPOSE: ....

 # OF MEETINGS TO COMPLETE THIS BADGE: .... **JOURNEY CONNECTION(S):** .... ☐ STEP 1 ☐ STEP 2 ☐ STEP 3 ☐ STEP 4 ☐ STEP 5

LONG-TERM PLANNING:

FIELD TRIP/GUEST SPEAKER IDEAS:

STEP 1:   **TIME NEEDED:** .... **MINUTES**

ACTIVITY: .... **TO BE COMPLETED AT:** ☐ HOME ☐ MEETING ☐ EVENT ☐ FIELD TRIP

PREP/SUPPLIES NEEDED: **WHO'S RESPONSIBLE?**

(1) .... ☐ LEADER ☐ GIRL/VOLUNTEER: ....

(2) .... ☐ LEADER ☐ GIRL/VOLUNTEER: ....

(3) .... ☐ LEADER ☐ GIRL/VOLUNTEER: ....

(4) .... ☐ LEADER ☐ GIRL/VOLUNTEER: ....

(5) .... ☐ LEADER ☐ GIRL/VOLUNTEER: ....

ACTIVITY STEPS/NOTES:

LEADERSHIP KEYS: ☐ DISCOVER ☐ CONNECT ☐ TAKE ACTION   **PROCESSES:** ☐ GIRL-LED ☐ LEARNING BY DOING ☐ COOPERATIVE LEARNING

STEP 2:   **TIME NEEDED:** .... **MINUTES**

ACTIVITY: .... **TO BE COMPLETED AT:** ☐ HOME ☐ MEETING ☐ EVENT ☐ FIELD TRIP

PREP/SUPPLIES NEEDED: **WHO'S RESPONSIBLE?**

(1) .... ☐ LEADER ☐ GIRL/VOLUNTEER: ....

(2) .... ☐ LEADER ☐ GIRL/VOLUNTEER: ....

(3) .... ☐ LEADER ☐ GIRL/VOLUNTEER: ....

(4) .... ☐ LEADER ☐ GIRL/VOLUNTEER: ....

(5) .... ☐ LEADER ☐ GIRL/VOLUNTEER: ....

ACTIVITY STEPS/NOTES:

LEADERSHIP KEYS: ☐ DISCOVER ☐ CONNECT ☐ TAKE ACTION   **PROCESSES:** ☐ GIRL-LED ☐ LEARNING BY DOING ☐ COOPERATIVE LEARNING

STEP 3:

TIME NEEDED: .... MINUTES

ACTIVITY: .... TO BE COMPLETED AT: ☐ HOME ☐ MEETING ☐ EVENT ☐ FIELD TRIP

PREP/SUPPLIES NEEDED: WHO'S RESPONSIBLE?

(1) .... ☐ LEADER ☐ GIRL/VOLUNTEER: ....

(2) .... ☐ LEADER ☐ GIRL/VOLUNTEER: ....

(3) .... ☐ LEADER ☐ GIRL/VOLUNTEER: ....

(4) .... ☐ LEADER ☐ GIRL/VOLUNTEER: ....

(5) .... ☐ LEADER ☐ GIRL/VOLUNTEER: ....

ACTIVITY STEPS/NOTES:

LEADERSHIP KEYS: ☐ DISCOVER ☐ CONNECT ☐ TAKE ACTION   PROCESSES: ☐ GIRL-LED ☐ LEARNING BY DOING ☐ COOPERATIVE LEARNING

STEP 4:

TIME NEEDED: .... MINUTES

ACTIVITY: .... TO BE COMPLETED AT: ☐ HOME ☐ MEETING ☐ EVENT ☐ FIELD TRIP

PREP/SUPPLIES NEEDED: WHO'S RESPONSIBLE?

(1) .... ☐ LEADER ☐ GIRL/VOLUNTEER: ....

(2) .... ☐ LEADER ☐ GIRL/VOLUNTEER: ....

(3) .... ☐ LEADER ☐ GIRL/VOLUNTEER: ....

(4) .... ☐ LEADER ☐ GIRL/VOLUNTEER: ....

(5) .... ☐ LEADER ☐ GIRL/VOLUNTEER: ....

ACTIVITY STEPS/NOTES:

LEADERSHIP KEYS: ☐ DISCOVER ☐ CONNECT ☐ TAKE ACTION   PROCESSES: ☐ GIRL-LED ☐ LEARNING BY DOING ☐ COOPERATIVE LEARNING

STEP 5:

TIME NEEDED: .... MINUTES

ACTIVITY: .... TO BE COMPLETED AT: ☐ HOME ☐ MEETING ☐ EVENT ☐ FIELD TRIP

PREP/SUPPLIES NEEDED: WHO'S RESPONSIBLE?

(1) .... ☐ LEADER ☐ GIRL/VOLUNTEER: ....

(2) .... ☐ LEADER ☐ GIRL/VOLUNTEER: ....

(3) .... ☐ LEADER ☐ GIRL/VOLUNTEER: ....

(4) .... ☐ LEADER ☐ GIRL/VOLUNTEER: ....

(5) .... ☐ LEADER ☐ GIRL/VOLUNTEER: ....

ACTIVITY STEPS/NOTES:

LEADERSHIP KEYS: ☐ DISCOVER ☐ CONNECT ☐ TAKE ACTION   PROCESSES: ☐ GIRL-LED ☐ LEARNING BY DOING ☐ COOPERATIVE LEARNING

BADGE ACTIVITIES PLANNER

BADGE: ....

PURPOSE: ....

OF MEETINGS TO COMPLETE THIS BADGE: .... JOURNEY CONNECTION(S): .... ☐ STEP 1 ☐ STEP 2 ☐ STEP 3 ☐ STEP 4 ☐ STEP 5

LONG-TERM PLANNING:

FIELD TRIP/GUEST SPEAKER IDEAS:

STEP 1: .... TIME NEEDED: .... MINUTES

ACTIVITY: .... TO BE COMPLETED AT: ☐ HOME ☐ MEETING ☐ EVENT ☐ FIELD TRIP

PREP/SUPPLIES NEEDED: WHO'S RESPONSIBLE?

(1) .... ☐ LEADER ☐ GIRL/VOLUNTEER: ....

(2) .... ☐ LEADER ☐ GIRL/VOLUNTEER: ....

(3) .... ☐ LEADER ☐ GIRL/VOLUNTEER: ....

(4) .... ☐ LEADER ☐ GIRL/VOLUNTEER: ....

(5) .... ☐ LEADER ☐ GIRL/VOLUNTEER: ....

ACTIVITY STEPS/NOTES:

LEADERSHIP KEYS: ☐ DISCOVER ☐ CONNECT ☐ TAKE ACTION   PROCESSES: ☐ GIRL-LED ☐ LEARNING BY DOING ☐ COOPERATIVE LEARNING

STEP 2: .... TIME NEEDED: .... MINUTES

ACTIVITY: .... TO BE COMPLETED AT: ☐ HOME ☐ MEETING ☐ EVENT ☐ FIELD TRIP

PREP/SUPPLIES NEEDED: WHO'S RESPONSIBLE?

(1) .... ☐ LEADER ☐ GIRL/VOLUNTEER: ....

(2) .... ☐ LEADER ☐ GIRL/VOLUNTEER: ....

(3) .... ☐ LEADER ☐ GIRL/VOLUNTEER: ....

(4) .... ☐ LEADER ☐ GIRL/VOLUNTEER: ....

(5) .... ☐ LEADER ☐ GIRL/VOLUNTEER: ....

ACTIVITY STEPS/NOTES:

LEADERSHIP KEYS: ☐ DISCOVER ☐ CONNECT ☐ TAKE ACTION   PROCESSES: ☐ GIRL-LED ☐ LEARNING BY DOING ☐ COOPERATIVE LEARNING

STEP 3: TIME NEEDED: .... MINUTES

ACTIVITY: .... TO BE COMPLETED AT: ☐ HOME ☐ MEETING ☐ EVENT ☐ FIELD TRIP

PREP/SUPPLIES NEEDED: WHO'S RESPONSIBLE?

(1) .... ☐ LEADER ☐ GIRL/VOLUNTEER: ....

(2) .... ☐ LEADER ☐ GIRL/VOLUNTEER: ....

(3) .... ☐ LEADER ☐ GIRL/VOLUNTEER: ....

(4) .... ☐ LEADER ☐ GIRL/VOLUNTEER: ....

(5) .... ☐ LEADER ☐ GIRL/VOLUNTEER: ....

ACTIVITY STEPS/NOTES:

LEADERSHIP KEYS: ☐ DISCOVER ☐ CONNECT ☐ TAKE ACTION   PROCESSES: ☐ GIRL-LED ☐ LEARNING BY DOING ☐ COOPERATIVE LEARNING

STEP 4: TIME NEEDED: .... MINUTES

ACTIVITY: .... TO BE COMPLETED AT: ☐ HOME ☐ MEETING ☐ EVENT ☐ FIELD TRIP

PREP/SUPPLIES NEEDED: WHO'S RESPONSIBLE?

(1) .... ☐ LEADER ☐ GIRL/VOLUNTEER: ....

(2) .... ☐ LEADER ☐ GIRL/VOLUNTEER: ....

(3) .... ☐ LEADER ☐ GIRL/VOLUNTEER: ....

(4) .... ☐ LEADER ☐ GIRL/VOLUNTEER: ....

(5) .... ☐ LEADER ☐ GIRL/VOLUNTEER: ....

ACTIVITY STEPS/NOTES:

LEADERSHIP KEYS: ☐ DISCOVER ☐ CONNECT ☐ TAKE ACTION   PROCESSES: ☐ GIRL-LED ☐ LEARNING BY DOING ☐ COOPERATIVE LEARNING

STEP 5: TIME NEEDED: .... MINUTES

ACTIVITY: .... TO BE COMPLETED AT: ☐ HOME ☐ MEETING ☐ EVENT ☐ FIELD TRIP

PREP/SUPPLIES NEEDED: WHO'S RESPONSIBLE?

(1) .... ☐ LEADER ☐ GIRL/VOLUNTEER: ....

(2) .... ☐ LEADER ☐ GIRL/VOLUNTEER: ....

(3) .... ☐ LEADER ☐ GIRL/VOLUNTEER: ....

(4) .... ☐ LEADER ☐ GIRL/VOLUNTEER: ....

(5) .... ☐ LEADER ☐ GIRL/VOLUNTEER: ....

ACTIVITY STEPS/NOTES:

LEADERSHIP KEYS: ☐ DISCOVER ☐ CONNECT ☐ TAKE ACTION   PROCESSES: ☐ GIRL-LED ☐ LEARNING BY DOING ☐ COOPERATIVE LEARNING

TRACKER:

CUSTOMIZE THIS TRACKER TO MEET YOUR NEEDS! RECORD ATTENDANCE, DUES, BADGES, PRODUCT SALES, ETC.

TROOPS WITH 5-10 MEMBERS: LIST YOUR MEETINGS/DUES/PAPERWORK/BADGES/PRODUCTS IN THE FIRST COLUMN AND YOUR GIRL'S NAMES IN THE ANGLED COLUMN HEADERS.

TROOPS WITH 10+ MEMBERS: LIST YOUR GIRL'S NAMES IN THE FIRST COLUMN AND YOUR MEETINGS/DUES/PAPERWORK/BADGES/PRODUCTS IN THE ANGLED COLUMN HEADERS.

TRACKER:

CUSTOMIZE THIS TRACKER TO MEET YOUR NEEDS: RECORD ATTENDANCE, DUES, BADGES, PRODUCT SALES, ETC.
TROOPS WITH 5-10 MEMBERS: LIST YOUR MEETINGS/DUES/PAPERWORK/BADGES/PRODUCTS IN THE FIRST COLUMN AND YOUR GIRL'S NAMES IN THE ANGLED COLUMN HEADERS.
TROOPS WITH 10+ MEMBERS: LIST YOUR GIRL'S NAMES IN THE FIRST COLUMN AND YOUR MEETINGS/DUES/PAPERWORK/BADGES/PRODUCTS IN THE ANGLED COLUMN HEADERS.

TRACKER:

CUSTOMIZE THIS TRACKER TO MEET YOUR NEEDS! RECORD ATTENDANCE, DUES, BADGES, PRODUCT SALES, ETC.
TROOPS WITH 5-10 MEMBERS: LIST YOUR MEETINGS/DUES/PAPERWORK/BADGES/PRODUCTS IN THE FIRST COLUMN AND YOUR GIRL'S NAMES IN THE ANGLED COLUMN HEADERS.
TROOPS WITH 10+ MEMBERS: LIST YOUR GIRL'S NAMES IN THE FIRST COLUMN AND YOUR MEETINGS/DUES/PAPERWORK/BADGES/PRODUCTS IN THE ANGLED COLUMN HEADERS.

TRACKER:

CUSTOMIZE THIS TRACKER TO MEET YOUR NEEDS! RECORD ATTENDANCE, DUES, BADGES, PRODUCT SALES, ETC.
TROOPS WITH 5-10 MEMBERS: LIST YOUR MEETINGS/DUES/PAPERWORK/BADGES/PRODUCTS IN THE FIRST COLUMN AND YOUR GIRL'S NAMES IN THE ANGLED COLUMN HEADERS.
TROOPS WITH 10+ MEMBERS: LIST YOUR GIRL'S NAMES IN THE FIRST COLUMN AND YOUR MEETINGS/DUES/PAPERWORK/BADGES/PRODUCTS IN THE ANGLED COLUMN HEADERS.

TRACKER:

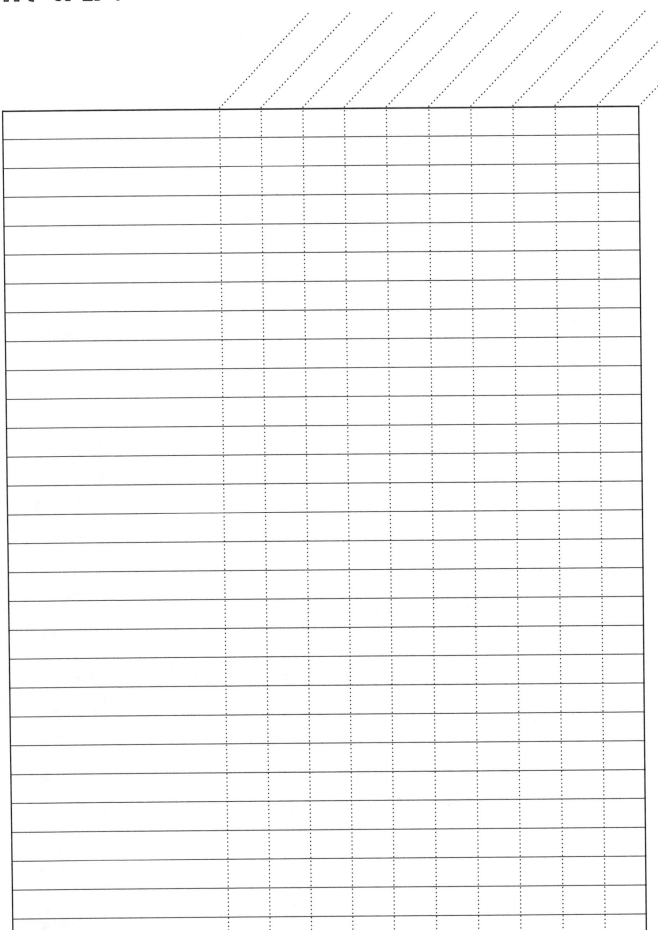

CUSTOMIZE THIS TRACKER TO MEET YOUR NEEDS! RECORD ATTENDANCE, DUES, BADGES, PRODUCT SALES, ETC.

TROOPS WITH 5-10 MEMBERS: LIST YOUR MEETINGS/DUES/PAPERWORK/BADGES/PRODUCTS IN THE FIRST COLUMN AND YOUR GIRL'S NAMES IN THE ANGLED COLUMN HEADERS.

TROOPS WITH 10+ MEMBERS: LIST YOUR GIRL'S NAMES IN THE FIRST COLUMN AND YOUR MEETINGS/DUES/PAPERWORK/BADGES/PRODUCTS IN THE ANGLED COLUMN HEADERS.

TRACKER:

CUSTOMIZE THIS TRACKER TO MEET YOUR NEEDS! RECORD ATTENDANCE, DUES, BADGES, PRODUCT SALES, ETC.
TROOPS WITH 5-10 MEMBERS: LIST YOUR MEETINGS/DUES/PAPERWORK/BADGES/PRODUCTS IN THE FIRST COLUMN AND YOUR GIRL'S NAMES IN THE ANGLED COLUMN HEADERS.
TROOPS WITH 10+ MEMBERS: LIST YOUR GIRL'S NAMES IN THE FIRST COLUMN AND YOUR MEETINGS/DUES/PAPERWORK/BADGES/PRODUCTS IN THE ANGLED COLUMN HEADERS.

TRACKER:

CUSTOMIZE THIS TRACKER TO MEET YOUR NEEDS! RECORD ATTENDANCE, DUES, BADGES, PRODUCT SALES, ETC.

TROOPS WITH 5-10 MEMBERS: LIST YOUR MEETINGS/DUES/PAPERWORK/BADGES/PRODUCTS IN THE FIRST COLUMN AND YOUR GIRL'S NAMES IN THE ANGLED COLUMN HEADERS.

TROOPS WITH 10+ MEMBERS: LIST YOUR GIRL'S NAMES IN THE FIRST COLUMN AND YOUR MEETINGS/DUES/PAPERWORK/BADGES/PRODUCTS IN THE ANGLED COLUMN HEADERS.

TRACKER:

CUSTOMIZE THIS TRACKER TO MEET YOUR NEEDS! RECORD ATTENDANCE, DUES, BADGES, PRODUCT SALES, ETC.
TROOPS WITH 5-10 MEMBERS: LIST YOUR MEETINGS/DUES/PAPERWORK/BADGES/PRODUCTS IN THE FIRST COLUMN AND YOUR GIRL'S NAMES IN THE ANGLED COLUMN HEADERS.
TROOPS WITH 10+ MEMBERS: LIST YOUR GIRL'S NAMES IN THE FIRST COLUMN AND YOUR MEETINGS/DUES/PAPERWORK/BADGES/PRODUCTS IN THE ANGLED COLUMN HEADERS.

TRACKER:

CUSTOMIZE THIS TRACKER TO MEET YOUR NEEDS! RECORD ATTENDANCE, DUES, BADGES, PRODUCT SALES, ETC.
TROOPS WITH 5-10 MEMBERS: LIST YOUR MEETINGS/DUES/PAPERWORK/BADGES/PRODUCTS IN THE FIRST COLUMN AND YOUR GIRL'S NAMES IN THE ANGLED COLUMN HEADERS.
TROOPS WITH 10+ MEMBERS: LIST YOUR GIRL'S NAMES IN THE FIRST COLUMN AND YOUR MEETINGS/DUES/PAPERWORK/BADGES/PRODUCTS IN THE ANGLED COLUMN HEADERS.

TRACKER:

CUSTOMIZE THIS TRACKER TO MEET YOUR NEEDS! RECORD ATTENDANCE, DUES, BADGES, PRODUCT SALES, ETC.

TROOPS WITH 5-10 MEMBERS: LIST YOUR MEETINGS/DUES/PAPERWORK/BADGES/PRODUCTS IN THE FIRST COLUMN AND YOUR GIRL'S NAMES IN THE ANGLED COLUMN HEADERS.

TROOPS WITH 10+ MEMBERS: LIST YOUR GIRL'S NAMES IN THE FIRST COLUMN AND YOUR MEETINGS/DUES/PAPERWORK/BADGES/PRODUCTS IN THE ANGLED COLUMN HEADERS.

TROOP DUES & BUDGET PLANNER

OF GIRLS: .... # OF VOLUNTEERS: .... # OF MEETINGS: .... NOTES:

TROOP EXPENSES   TOTAL TROOP EXPENSES: $ ....

PROGRAMS, EVENTS & FIELD TRIPS

(1) $........ X .... = $........	(11) $........ X .... = $........
(2) $........ X .... = $........	(12) $........ X .... = $........
(3) $........ X .... = $........	(13) $........ X .... = $........
(4) $........ X .... = $........	(14) $........ X .... = $........
(5) $........ X .... = $........	(15) $........ X .... = $........
(6) $........ X .... = $........	(16) $........ X .... = $........
(7) $........ X .... = $........	(17) $........ X .... = $........
(8) $........ X .... = $........	(18) $........ X .... = $........
(9) $........ X .... = $........	(19) $........ X .... = $........
(10) $........ X .... = $........	(20) $........ X .... = $........

TOTAL FOR PROGRAMS, EVENTS & FIELD TRIPS: $

UNIFORMS, BADGES & INSIGNIA

UNIFORMS $........ X .... = $........	FUN PATCHES $........ X .... = $........
GIRL SCOUTING GUIDES $........ X .... = $........	OTHER: $........ X .... = $........
JOURNEYS $........ X .... = $........	OTHER: $........ X .... = $........
BADGES $........ X .... = $........	OTHER: $........ X .... = $........

TOTAL FOR UNIFORMS, BADGES & INSIGNIA: $

SUPPLIES, SNACKS & OTHER EXPENSES

ANNUAL MEMBERSHIP FEES $........ X .... = $........	COOKIE BOOTH SETUP $........ X .... = $........
SERVICE UNIT DUES $........ X .... = $........	CEREMONIES/CELEBRATIONS $........ X .... = $........
ANNUAL FUND DONATIONS $........ X .... = $........	CHARITABLE CONTRIBUTIONS $........ X .... = $........
TROOP NECESSITIES $........ X .... = $........	OTHER: $........ X .... = $........
BADGE ACTIVITY SUPPLIES $........ X .... = $........	OTHER: $........ X .... = $........
SNACKS $........ X .... = $........	OTHER: $........ X .... = $........

TOTAL FOR SUPPLIES, SNACKS & OTHER EXPENSES: $

PARENT/GUARDIAN CONTRIBUTIONS

TOTAL PARENT/GUARDIAN CONTRIBUTIONS: $ ....

PROGRAMS, EVENTS & FIELD TRIPS: $ .... FUN PATCHES: $ .... BADGE ACTIVITY SUPPLIES: $ ....

UNIFORMS: $ .... ANNUAL MEMBERSHIP FEES: $ .... SNACKS: $ ....

GIRL SCOUTING GUIDES: $ .... SERVICE UNIT DUES: $ .... COOKIE BOOTH SETUP: $ ....

JOURNEYS: $ .... ANNUAL FUND DONATIONS: $ .... OTHER: ....

BADGES: $ .... TROOP NECESSITIES: $ .... OTHER: ....

TOTAL TROOP EXPENSES ($ ....) MINUS TOTAL CONTRIBUTIONS FROM PARENTS/GUARDIANS ($ ....) = REMAINING TROOP EXPENSES ($ ....)

TROOP INCOME

TOTAL ESTIMATED TROOP INCOME: $ ....

FALL PRODUCT SALES ☐ TROOP WILL PARTICIPATE ☐ TROOP WILL NOT PARTICIPATE

TROOP PROFIT PER SALE: .... # OF GIRLS PARTICIPATING: .... SALES REQUIRED TO COVER REMAINING TROOP EXPENSES: $ .... ☐ ACHIEVABLE ☐ UNREALISTIC

TOTAL ESTIMATED FALL PRODUCT PROFIT: $ .... GROSS SALES OUR TROOP MUST MAKE TO ACHIEVE THIS ESTIMATED PROFIT: $ ....

COOKIE SALES ☐ TROOP WILL PARTICIPATE ☐ TROOP WILL NOT PARTICIPATE

TROOP PROFIT PER BOX: $ .... # OF GIRLS PARTICIPATING: .... SALES REQUIRED TO COVER REMAINING TROOP EXPENSES: .... ☐ ACHIEVEABLE ☐ UNREALISTIC

TOTAL ESTIMATED COOKIE PROFIT: $ .... # OF BOXES OUR TROOP MUST SELL TO ACHIEVE THIS ESTIMATED PROFIT: ....

OTHER COUNCIL-APPROVED MONEY-EARNING ACTIVITIES ☐ TROOP WILL PARTICIPATE ☐ TROOP WILL NOT PARTICIPATE

(1) .... : $ .... (2) .... : $ .... (3) .... : $ ....

TOTAL ESTIMATED PROFIT FROM OTHER COUNCIL-APPROVED MONEY-EARNING ACTIVITIES: $ ....

TROOP DUES

STARTING ACCOUNT BALANCE: $ .... ☐ 100% IS RESERVED FOR A TRIP, ETC. ☐ 100% CAN BE USED TO COVER EXPENSES ☐ $ .... CAN BE USED TO COVER EXPENSES

TROOP DUES CALCULATOR:

$ .... + $ .... + $ .... = $ .... - $ .... = $ ....
AVAILABLE FUNDS FROM ACCOUNT BALANCE | PARENT/GUARDIAN CONTRIBUTIONS | TOTAL ESTIMATED TROOP INCOME | | TOTAL TROOP EXPENSES | TOTAL TROOP DUES

TOTAL TROOP DUES ($ ....) DIVIDED BY THE NUMBER OF GIRLS (..........) = TROOP DUES PER GIRL ($ ....)

TROOP DUES WILL BE COLLECTED ☐ UPFRONT ☐ AT EACH MEETING (TROOP DUES PER GIRL DIVIDED BY # OF MEETINGS = $ ....)

NOTES:

TROOP FINANCES

CHECKING ACCOUNT DETAILS

STARTING BALANCE AS OF ....../......./....... : $..................

BANK: .... LOCATION: .... HOURS: ....

ACCOUNT NUMBER: .... ROUTING NUMBER: .... DEBIT CARD NUMBER: .... CVV: ....

NOTES: ....

DATE	CHECK/DEBIT	DESCRIPTION	WITHDRAWAL	DEPOSIT	BALANCE
	☐ CHECK # ☐ DEBIT CARD				
	☐ CHECK # ☐ DEBIT CARD				
	☐ CHECK # ☐ DEBIT CARD				
	☐ CHECK # ☐ DEBIT CARD				
	☐ CHECK # ☐ DEBIT CARD				
	☐ CHECK # ☐ DEBIT CARD				
	☐ CHECK # ☐ DEBIT CARD				
	☐ CHECK # ☐ DEBIT CARD				
	☐ CHECK # ☐ DEBIT CARD				
	☐ CHECK # ☐ DEBIT CARD				
	☐ CHECK # ☐ DEBIT CARD				
	☐ CHECK # ☐ DEBIT CARD				
	☐ CHECK # ☐ DEBIT CARD				
	☐ CHECK # ☐ DEBIT CARD				
	☐ CHECK # ☐ DEBIT CARD				
	☐ CHECK # ☐ DEBIT CARD				
	☐ CHECK # ☐ DEBIT CARD				
	☐ CHECK # ☐ DEBIT CARD				
	☐ CHECK # ☐ DEBIT CARD				
	☐ CHECK # ☐ DEBIT CARD				

"We do not need magic to change the world, we carry all the power we need inside ourselves already."
— JK ROWLING

DATE	CHECK/DEBIT	DESCRIPTION	WITHDRAWAL	DEPOSIT	BALANCE
	☐ CHECK # ☐ DEBIT CARD				
	☐ CHECK # ☐ DEBIT CARD				
	☐ CHECK # ☐ DEBIT CARD				
	☐ CHECK # ☐ DEBIT CARD				
	☐ CHECK # ☐ DEBIT CARD				
	☐ CHECK # ☐ DEBIT CARD				
	☐ CHECK # ☐ DEBIT CARD				
	☐ CHECK # ☐ DEBIT CARD				
	☐ CHECK # ☐ DEBIT CARD				
	☐ CHECK # ☐ DEBIT CARD				
	☐ CHECK # ☐ DEBIT CARD				
	☐ CHECK # ☐ DEBIT CARD				
	☐ CHECK # ☐ DEBIT CARD				
	☐ CHECK # ☐ DEBIT CARD				
	☐ CHECK # ☐ DEBIT CARD				
	☐ CHECK # ☐ DEBIT CARD				
	☐ CHECK # ☐ DEBIT CARD				
	☐ CHECK # ☐ DEBIT CARD				
	☐ CHECK # ☐ DEBIT CARD				
	☐ CHECK # ☐ DEBIT CARD				
	☐ CHECK # ☐ DEBIT CARD				
	☐ CHECK # ☐ DEBIT CARD				
	☐ CHECK # ☐ DEBIT CARD				
	☐ CHECK # ☐ DEBIT CARD				

TROOP LEADER TAX-DEDUCTIBLE EXPENSES

DATE	EXPENSE	COST	DATE	EXPENSE	COST
DATE	EXPENSE	COST	DATE	EXPENSE	COST

TROOP LEADER TAX-DEDUCTIBLE MILEAGE

DATE	PURPOSE	MILES	DATE	PURPOSE	MILES

COOKIE BOOTH PLANNER

TROOP COOKIE MANAGER(S): ....

COOKIE BOOTH NOTES:

DATE & TIME	COOKIE BOOTH LOCATION	VOLUNTEERS		GIRLS	
M T W TH F SAT SUN		(1)	(1)	(3)	
		(2)	(2)	(4)	
M T W TH F SAT SUN		(1)	(1)	(3)	
		(2)	(2)	(4)	
M T W TH F SAT SUN		(1)	(1)	(3)	
		(2)	(2)	(4)	
M T W TH F SAT SUN		(1)	(1)	(3)	
		(2)	(2)	(4)	
M T W TH F SAT SUN		(1)	(1)	(3)	
		(2)	(2)	(4)	
M T W TH F SAT SUN		(1)	(1)	(3)	
		(2)	(2)	(4)	
M T W TH F SAT SUN		(1)	(1)	(3)	
		(2)	(2)	(4)	
M T W TH F SAT SUN		(1)	(1)	(3)	
		(2)	(2)	(4)	

"Learn from the mistakes of others. You can't live long enough to make them all yourself."
ELEANOR ROOSEVELT

COOKIE BOOTH NOTES:

DATE & TIME	COOKIE BOOTH LOCATION	VOLUNTEERS		GIRLS	
		(1)	(1)	(3)	
M T W TH F SAT SUN		(2)	(2)	(4)	
		(1)	(1)	(3)	
M T W TH F SAT SUN		(2)	(2)	(4)	
		(1)	(1)	(3)	
M T W TH F SAT SUN		(2)	(2)	(4)	
		(1)	(1)	(3)	
M T W TH F SAT SUN		(2)	(2)	(4)	
		(1)	(1)	(3)	
M T W TH F SAT SUN		(2)	(2)	(4)	
		(1)	(1)	(3)	
M T W TH F SAT SUN		(2)	(2)	(4)	
		(1)	(1)	(3)	
M T W TH F SAT SUN		(2)	(2)	(4)	
		(1)	(1)	(3)	
M T W TH F SAT SUN		(2)	(2)	(4)	

COOKIE BOOTH SALES TRACKER

COOKIE BOOTH LOCATION: _____   **TOTAL CASH & CREDIT CARD SALES:** $ _____

DATE: ___/___/___   **STARTING TIME:** _____   **ENDING TIME:** _____   **VOLUNTEERS:** _____

	PRICE PER BOX	STARTING # OF BOXES	ENDING # OF BOXES	BOXES SOLD	CASH SALES	CREDIT CARD SALES
THIN MINTS	$				$	$
SAMOAS / CARAMEL DELITES	$				$	$
TAGALONGS / PEANUT BUTTER PATTIES	$				$	$
TREFOILS / SHORTBREAD	$				$	$
DO-SI-DOS / PEANUT BUTTER SANDWICH	$				$	$
SAVANNAH SMILES	$				$	$
TOFFEE-TASTIC	$				$	$
THANKS-A-LOT	$				$	$
S'MORES	$				$	$
LEMONADES	$				$	$
CARAMEL CHOCOLATE CHIP	$				$	$
TOTALS:		_____	_____	_____	$ _____	$ _____
		STARTING # OF BOXES	ENDING # OF BOXES	BOXES SOLD	CASH SALES	CREDIT CARD SALES

STARTING # OF BOXES (_____) MINUS ENDING # OF BOXES (_____) = TOTAL BOXES SOLD (_____) ☐ SAME AS ABOVE (YAY!) ☐ DIFFERENT FROM ABOVE (UH-OH)

ENDING CASH ($_____) MINUS STARTING CASH ($_____) = TOTAL CASH SALES ($_____) ☐ SAME AS ABOVE (YAY!) ☐ DIFFERENT FROM ABOVE (UH-OH)

COOKIE BOOTH HOURS

GIRL	START TIME	END TIME	TOTAL HOURS	BOXES SOLD	GIRL	START TIME	END TIME	TOTAL HOURS	BOXES SOLD

NOTES:

TOTAL ESTIMATED TROOP PROFIT FROM THIS COOKIE BOOTH: $ _____

"There are still many causes worth sacrificing for, so much history yet to be made."
MICHELLE OBAMA

COOKIE BOOTH LOCATION:

TOTAL CASH & CREDIT CARD SALES: $ ....

DATE: ..../..../.... STARTING TIME: .... ENDING TIME: .... VOLUNTEERS: ....

	PRICE PER BOX	STARTING # OF BOXES	ENDING # OF BOXES	BOXES SOLD	CASH SALES	CREDIT CARD SALES
THIN MINTS	$				$	$
SAMOAS / CARAMEL DELITES	$				$	$
TAGALONGS / PEANUT BUTTER PATTIES	$				$	$
TREFOILS / SHORTBREAD	$				$	$
DO-SI-DOS / PEANUT BUTTER SANDWICH	$				$	$
SAVANNAH SMILES	$				$	$
TOFFEE-TASTIC	$				$	$
THANKS-A-LOT	$				$	$
S'MORES	$				$	$
LEMONADES	$				$	$
CARAMEL CHOCOLATE CHIP	$				$	$
TOTALS:		....	....	....	$............	$............
		STARTING # OF BOXES	ENDING # OF BOXES	BOXES SOLD	CASH SALES	CREDIT CARD SALES

STARTING # OF BOXES (............) MINUS ENDING # OF BOXES (............) = TOTAL BOXES SOLD (............) ☐ SAME AS ABOVE (YAY!) ☐ DIFFERENT FROM ABOVE (UH-OH)

ENDING CASH ($............) MINUS STARTING CASH ($............) = TOTAL CASH SALES ($............) ☐ SAME AS ABOVE (YAY!) ☐ DIFFERENT FROM ABOVE (UH-OH)

COOKIE BOOTH HOURS

GIRL	START TIME	END TIME	TOTAL HOURS	BOXES SOLD	GIRL	START TIME	END TIME	TOTAL HOURS	BOXES SOLD

NOTES:

TOTAL ESTIMATED TROOP PROFIT FROM THIS COOKIE BOOTH: $ ....

COOKIE BOOTH SALES TRACKER

COOKIE BOOTH LOCATION: _____ TOTAL CASH & CREDIT CARD SALES: $ _____

DATE: ___/___/___ STARTING TIME: _____ ENDING TIME: _____ VOLUNTEERS: _____

	PRICE PER BOX	STARTING # OF BOXES	ENDING # OF BOXES	BOXES SOLD	CASH SALES	CREDIT CARD SALES
THIN MINTS	$				$	$
SAMOAS / CARAMEL DELITES	$				$	$
TAGALONGS / PEANUT BUTTER PATTIES	$				$	$
TREFOILS / SHORTBREAD	$				$	$
DO-SI-DOS / PEANUT BUTTER SANDWICH	$				$	$
SAVANNAH SMILES	$				$	$
TOFFEE-TASTIC	$				$	$
THANKS-A-LOT	$				$	$
S'MORES	$				$	$
LEMONADES	$				$	$
CARAMEL CHOCOLATE CHIP	$				$	$
TOTALS:		_____	_____	_____	$ _____	$ _____
		STARTING # OF BOXES	ENDING # OF BOXES	BOXES SOLD	CASH SALES	CREDIT CARD SALES

STARTING # OF BOXES (_____) MINUS ENDING # OF BOXES (_____) = TOTAL BOXES SOLD (_____) ☐ SAME AS ABOVE (YAY!) ☐ DIFFERENT FROM ABOVE (UH-OH)

ENDING CASH ($_____) MINUS STARTING CASH ($_____) = TOTAL CASH SALES ($_____) ☐ SAME AS ABOVE (YAY!) ☐ DIFFERENT FROM ABOVE (UH-OH)

COOKIE BOOTH HOURS

GIRL	START TIME	END TIME	TOTAL HOURS	BOXES SOLD	GIRL	START TIME	END TIME	TOTAL HOURS	BOXES SOLD

NOTES:

TOTAL ESTIMATED TROOP PROFIT FROM THIS COOKIE BOOTH: $ _____

"If you don't know what you're here to do, then just do some good."
— MAYA ANGELOU

COOKIE BOOTH LOCATION:

TOTAL CASH & CREDIT CARD SALES: $ ....

DATE: ...../...../..... STARTING TIME: .... ENDING TIME: .... VOLUNTEERS: ....

	PRICE PER BOX	STARTING # OF BOXES	ENDING # OF BOXES	BOXES SOLD	CASH SALES	CREDIT CARD SALES
THIN MINTS	$				$	$
SAMOAS / CARAMEL DELITES	$				$	$
TAGALONGS / PEANUT BUTTER PATTIES	$				$	$
TREFOILS / SHORTBREAD	$				$	$
DO-SI-DOS / PEANUT BUTTER SANDWICH	$				$	$
SAVANNAH SMILES	$				$	$
TOFFEE-TASTIC	$				$	$
THANKS-A-LOT	$				$	$
S'MORES	$				$	$
LEMONADES	$				$	$
CARAMEL CHOCOLATE CHIP	$				$	$
TOTALS:		STARTING # OF BOXES	ENDING # OF BOXES	BOXES SOLD	$ CASH SALES	$ CREDIT CARD SALES

STARTING # OF BOXES (..........) MINUS ENDING # OF BOXES (..........) = TOTAL BOXES SOLD (..........) ☐ SAME AS ABOVE (YAY!) ☐ DIFFERENT FROM ABOVE (UH-OH)

ENDING CASH ($..........) MINUS STARTING CASH ($..........) = TOTAL CASH SALES ($..........) ☐ SAME AS ABOVE (YAY!) ☐ DIFFERENT FROM ABOVE (UH-OH)

COOKIE BOOTH HOURS

GIRL	START TIME	END TIME	TOTAL HOURS	BOXES SOLD	GIRL	START TIME	END TIME	TOTAL HOURS	BOXES SOLD

NOTES:

TOTAL ESTIMATED TROOP PROFIT FROM THIS COOKIE BOOTH: $ ....

COOKIE BOOTH SALES TRACKER

COOKIE BOOTH LOCATION: _____   TOTAL CASH & CREDIT CARD SALES: $ _____

DATE: ___/___/___   STARTING TIME: _____   ENDING TIME: _____   VOLUNTEERS: _____

	PRICE PER BOX	STARTING # OF BOXES	ENDING # OF BOXES	BOXES SOLD	CASH SALES	CREDIT CARD SALES
THIN MINTS	$				$	$
SAMOAS / CARAMEL DELITES	$				$	$
TAGALONGS / PEANUT BUTTER PATTIES	$				$	$
TREFOILS / SHORTBREAD	$				$	$
DO-SI-DOS / PEANUT BUTTER SANDWICH	$				$	$
SAVANNAH SMILES	$				$	$
TOFFEE-TASTIC	$				$	$
THANKS-A-LOT	$				$	$
S'MORES	$				$	$
LEMONADES	$				$	$
CARAMEL CHOCOLATE CHIP	$				$	$
TOTALS:		_____	_____	_____	$_____	$_____
		STARTING # OF BOXES	ENDING # OF BOXES	BOXES SOLD	CASH SALES	CREDIT CARD SALES

STARTING # OF BOXES (_____) MINUS ENDING # OF BOXES (_____) = TOTAL BOXES SOLD (_____) ☐ SAME AS ABOVE (YAY!) ☐ DIFFERENT FROM ABOVE (UH-OH)

ENDING CASH ($_____) MINUS STARTING CASH ($_____) = TOTAL CASH SALES ($_____) ☐ SAME AS ABOVE (YAY!) ☐ DIFFERENT FROM ABOVE (UH-OH)

COOKIE BOOTH HOURS

GIRL	START TIME	END TIME	TOTAL HOURS	BOXES SOLD	GIRL	START TIME	END TIME	TOTAL HOURS	BOXES SOLD

NOTES:

TOTAL ESTIMATED TROOP PROFIT FROM THIS COOKIE BOOTH: $ _____

"What you do makes a difference, and you have to decide what kind of difference you want to make."
— JANE GOODALL

COOKIE BOOTH LOCATION:

TOTAL CASH & CREDIT CARD SALES: $ ....

DATE: ...../...../.....   STARTING TIME: ....   ENDING TIME: ....   VOLUNTEERS: ....

	PRICE PER BOX	STARTING # OF BOXES	ENDING # OF BOXES	BOXES SOLD	CASH SALES	CREDIT CARD SALES
THIN MINTS	$				$	$
SAMOAS / CARAMEL DELITES	$				$	$
TAGALONGS / PEANUT BUTTER PATTIES	$				$	$
TREFOILS / SHORTBREAD	$				$	$
DO-SI-DOS / PEANUT BUTTER SANDWICH	$				$	$
SAVANNAH SMILES	$				$	$
TOFFEE-TASTIC	$				$	$
THANKS-A-LOT	$				$	$
S'MORES	$				$	$
LEMONADES	$				$	$
CARAMEL CHOCOLATE CHIP	$				$	$
TOTALS:		....	....	....	$	$ ....
		STARTING # OF BOXES	ENDING # OF BOXES	BOXES SOLD	CASH SALES	CREDIT CARD SALES

STARTING # OF BOXES (..........) MINUS ENDING # OF BOXES (..........) = TOTAL BOXES SOLD (..........) ☐ SAME AS ABOVE (YAY!) ☐ DIFFERENT FROM ABOVE (UH-OH)

ENDING CASH ($..........) MINUS STARTING CASH ($..........) = TOTAL CASH SALES ($..........) ☐ SAME AS ABOVE (YAY!) ☐ DIFFERENT FROM ABOVE (UH-OH)

COOKIE BOOTH HOURS

GIRL	START TIME	END TIME	TOTAL HOURS	BOXES SOLD	GIRL	START TIME	END TIME	TOTAL HOURS	BOXES SOLD

NOTES:

TOTAL ESTIMATED TROOP PROFIT FROM THIS COOKIE BOOTH: $ ....

COOKIE BOOTH SALES TRACKER

COOKIE BOOTH LOCATION: _____   TOTAL CASH & CREDIT CARD SALES: $ _____

DATE: ___/___/___   STARTING TIME: _____   ENDING TIME: _____   VOLUNTEERS: _____

	PRICE PER BOX	STARTING # OF BOXES	ENDING # OF BOXES	BOXES SOLD	CASH SALES	CREDIT CARD SALES
THIN MINTS	$				$	$
SAMOAS / CARAMEL DELITES	$				$	$
TAGALONGS / PEANUT BUTTER PATTIES	$				$	$
TREFOILS / SHORTBREAD	$				$	$
DO-SI-DOS / PEANUT BUTTER SANDWICH	$				$	$
SAVANNAH SMILES	$				$	$
TOFFEE-TASTIC	$				$	$
THANKS-A-LOT	$				$	$
S'MORES	$				$	$
LEMONADES	$				$	$
CARAMEL CHOCOLATE CHIP	$				$	$
TOTALS:		_____	_____	_____	$ _____	$ _____
		STARTING # OF BOXES	ENDING # OF BOXES	BOXES SOLD	CASH SALES	CREDIT CARD SALES

STARTING # OF BOXES (_____) MINUS ENDING # OF BOXES (_____) = TOTAL BOXES SOLD (_____) ☐ SAME AS ABOVE (YAY!) ☐ DIFFERENT FROM ABOVE (UH-OH)

ENDING CASH ($_____) MINUS STARTING CASH ($_____) = TOTAL CASH SALES ($_____) ☐ SAME AS ABOVE (YAY!) ☐ DIFFERENT FROM ABOVE (UH-OH)

COOKIE BOOTH HOURS

GIRL	START TIME	END TIME	TOTAL HOURS	BOXES SOLD	GIRL	START TIME	END TIME	TOTAL HOURS	BOXES SOLD

NOTES:

TOTAL ESTIMATED TROOP PROFIT FROM THIS COOKIE BOOTH: $ _____

"A voice is a human gift; it should be cherished and used. ...Powerlessness and silence go together."
MARGARET ATWOOD

COOKIE BOOTH LOCATION:

TOTAL CASH & CREDIT CARD SALES: $ ....

DATE: ...../...../...... STARTING TIME: .... ENDING TIME: .... VOLUNTEERS: ....

	PRICE PER BOX	STARTING # OF BOXES	ENDING # OF BOXES	BOXES SOLD	CASH SALES	CREDIT CARD SALES
THIN MINTS	$				$	$
SAMOAS / CARAMEL DELITES	$				$	$
TAGALONGS / PEANUT BUTTER PATTIES	$				$	$
TREFOILS / SHORTBREAD	$				$	$
DO-SI-DOS / PEANUT BUTTER SANDWICH	$				$	$
SAVANNAH SMILES	$				$	$
TOFFEE-TASTIC	$				$	$
THANKS-A-LOT	$				$	$
S'MORES	$				$	$
LEMONADES	$				$	$
CARAMEL CHOCOLATE CHIP	$				$	$
TOTALS:		STARTING # OF BOXES	ENDING # OF BOXES	BOXES SOLD	$ CASH SALES	$ CREDIT CARD SALES

STARTING # OF BOXES (..........) MINUS ENDING # OF BOXES (..........) = TOTAL BOXES SOLD (..........) ☐ SAME AS ABOVE (YAY!) ☐ DIFFERENT FROM ABOVE (UH-OH)

ENDING CASH ($..........) MINUS STARTING CASH ($..........) = TOTAL CASH SALES ($..........) ☐ SAME AS ABOVE (YAY!) ☐ DIFFERENT FROM ABOVE (UH-OH)

COOKIE BOOTH HOURS

GIRL	START TIME	END TIME	TOTAL HOURS	BOXES SOLD	GIRL	START TIME	END TIME	TOTAL HOURS	BOXES SOLD

NOTES:

TOTAL ESTIMATED TROOP PROFIT FROM THIS COOKIE BOOTH: $ ....

COOKIE BOOTH SALES TRACKER

COOKIE BOOTH LOCATION: .... TOTAL CASH & CREDIT CARD SALES: $ ....

DATE: ...../...../..... STARTING TIME: .... ENDING TIME: .... VOLUNTEERS: ....

	PRICE PER BOX	STARTING # OF BOXES	ENDING # OF BOXES	BOXES SOLD	CASH SALES	CREDIT CARD SALES
THIN MINTS	$				$	$
SAMOAS / CARAMEL DELITES	$				$	$
TAGALONGS / PEANUT BUTTER PATTIES	$				$	$
TREFOILS / SHORTBREAD	$				$	$
DO-SI-DOS / PEANUT BUTTER SANDWICH	$				$	$
SAVANNAH SMILES	$				$	$
TOFFEE-TASTIC	$				$	$
THANKS-A-LOT	$				$	$
S'MORES	$				$	$
LEMONADES	$				$	$
CARAMEL CHOCOLATE CHIP	$				$	$
TOTALS:		....	....	....	$	$ ....
		STARTING # OF BOXES	ENDING # OF BOXES	BOXES SOLD	CASH SALES	CREDIT CARD SALES

STARTING # OF BOXES (..........) MINUS ENDING # OF BOXES (..........) = TOTAL BOXES SOLD (..........) ☐ SAME AS ABOVE (YAY!) ☐ DIFFERENT FROM ABOVE (UH-OH)

ENDING CASH ($..........) MINUS STARTING CASH ($..........) = TOTAL CASH SALES ($..........) ☐ SAME AS ABOVE (YAY!) ☐ DIFFERENT FROM ABOVE (UH-OH)

COOKIE BOOTH HOURS

GIRL	START TIME	END TIME	TOTAL HOURS	BOXES SOLD	GIRL	START TIME	END TIME	TOTAL HOURS	BOXES SOLD

NOTES:

TOTAL ESTIMATED TROOP PROFIT FROM THIS COOKIE BOOTH: $ ....

"We are never really happy until we try to brighten the lives of others."
— HELEN KELLER

COOKIE BOOTH LOCATION:

TOTAL CASH & CREDIT CARD SALES: $ ....

DATE: ...../...../..... STARTING TIME: .... ENDING TIME: .... VOLUNTEERS: ....

	PRICE PER BOX	STARTING # OF BOXES	ENDING # OF BOXES	BOXES SOLD	CASH SALES	CREDIT CARD SALES
THIN MINTS	$				$	$
SAMOAS / CARAMEL DELITES	$				$	$
TAGALONGS / PEANUT BUTTER PATTIES	$				$	$
TREFOILS / SHORTBREAD	$				$	$
DO-SI-DOS / PEANUT BUTTER SANDWICH	$				$	$
SAVANNAH SMILES	$				$	$
TOFFEE-TASTIC	$				$	$
THANKS-A-LOT	$				$	$
S'MORES	$				$	$
LEMONADES	$				$	$
CARAMEL CHOCOLATE CHIP	$				$	$
TOTALS:		....	....	....	$............	$............
		STARTING # OF BOXES	ENDING # OF BOXES	BOXES SOLD	CASH SALES	CREDIT CARD SALES

STARTING # OF BOXES (..........) MINUS ENDING # OF BOXES (..........) = TOTAL BOXES SOLD (..........) ☐ SAME AS ABOVE (YAY!) ☐ DIFFERENT FROM ABOVE (UH-OH)

ENDING CASH ($..........) MINUS STARTING CASH ($..........) = TOTAL CASH SALES ($..........) ☐ SAME AS ABOVE (YAY!) ☐ DIFFERENT FROM ABOVE (UH-OH)

COOKIE BOOTH HOURS

GIRL	START TIME	END TIME	TOTAL HOURS	BOXES SOLD	GIRL	START TIME	END TIME	TOTAL HOURS	BOXES SOLD

NOTES:

TOTAL ESTIMATED TROOP PROFIT FROM THIS COOKIE BOOTH: $ ....

TRACKER:

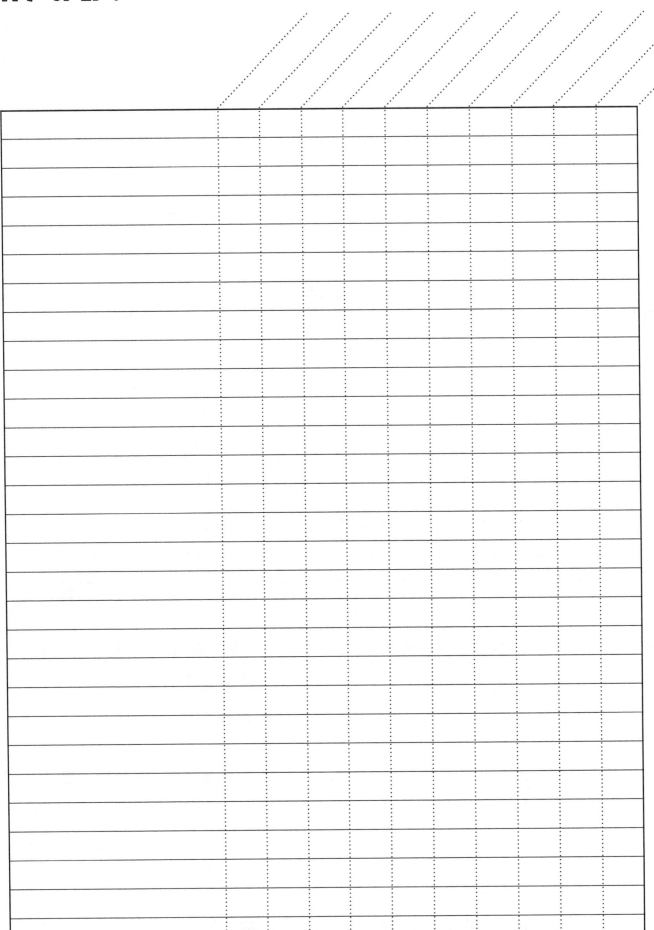

CUSTOMIZE THIS TRACKER TO MEET YOUR NEEDS! RECORD ATTENDANCE, DUES, BADGES, PRODUCT SALES, ETC.

TROOPS WITH 5-10 MEMBERS: LIST YOUR MEETINGS/DUES/PAPERWORK/BADGES/PRODUCTS IN THE FIRST COLUMN AND YOUR GIRL'S NAMES IN THE ANGLED COLUMN HEADERS.

TROOPS WITH 10+ MEMBERS: LIST YOUR GIRL'S NAMES IN THE FIRST COLUMN AND YOUR MEETINGS/DUES/PAPERWORK/BADGES/PRODUCTS IN THE ANGLED COLUMN HEADERS.

TRACKER:

CUSTOMIZE THIS TRACKER TO MEET YOUR NEEDS! RECORD ATTENDANCE, DUES, BADGES, PRODUCT SALES, ETC.

TROOPS WITH 5-10 MEMBERS: LIST YOUR MEETINGS/DUES/PAPERWORK/BADGES/PRODUCTS IN THE FIRST COLUMN AND YOUR GIRL'S NAMES IN THE ANGLED COLUMN HEADERS.

TROOPS WITH 10+ MEMBERS: LIST YOUR GIRL'S NAMES IN THE FIRST COLUMN AND YOUR MEETINGS/DUES/PAPERWORK/BADGES/PRODUCTS IN THE ANGLED COLUMN HEADERS.

TRACKER:

CUSTOMIZE THIS TRACKER TO MEET YOUR NEEDS! RECORD ATTENDANCE, DUES, BADGES, PRODUCT SALES, ETC.

TROOPS WITH 5-10 MEMBERS: LIST YOUR MEETINGS/DUES/PAPERWORK/BADGES/PRODUCTS IN THE FIRST COLUMN AND YOUR GIRL'S NAMES IN THE ANGLED COLUMN HEADERS.

TROOPS WITH 10+ MEMBERS: LIST YOUR GIRL'S NAMES IN THE FIRST COLUMN AND YOUR MEETINGS/DUES/PAPERWORK/BADGES/PRODUCTS IN THE ANGLED COLUMN HEADERS.

TRACKER:

CUSTOMIZE THIS TRACKER TO MEET YOUR NEEDS! RECORD ATTENDANCE, DUES, BADGES, PRODUCT SALES, ETC.
TROOPS WITH 5-10 MEMBERS: LIST YOUR MEETINGS/DUES/PAPERWORK/BADGES/PRODUCTS IN THE FIRST COLUMN AND YOUR GIRL'S NAMES IN THE ANGLED COLUMN HEADERS.
TROOPS WITH 10+ MEMBERS: LIST YOUR GIRL'S NAMES IN THE FIRST COLUMN AND YOUR MEETINGS/DUES/PAPERWORK/BADGES/PRODUCTS IN THE ANGLED COLUMN HEADERS.

VOLUNTEER SIGN-UP

THANK YOU!

NOTES FOR VOLUNTEERS:

DATE & TIME	MEETING / EVENT	# OF VOLUNTEERS NEEDED	VOLUNTEER NAMES & PHONE NUMBERS
M T W TH F SAT SUN	☐ MEETING ☐ COOKIE BOOTH ☐ EVENT:		
M T W TH F SAT SUN	☐ MEETING ☐ COOKIE BOOTH ☐ EVENT:		
M T W TH F SAT SUN	☐ MEETING ☐ COOKIE BOOTH ☐ EVENT:		
M T W TH F SAT SUN	☐ MEETING ☐ COOKIE BOOTH ☐ EVENT:		
M T W TH F SAT SUN	☐ MEETING ☐ COOKIE BOOTH ☐ EVENT:		
M T W TH F SAT SUN	☐ MEETING ☐ COOKIE BOOTH ☐ EVENT:		
M T W TH F SAT SUN	☐ MEETING ☐ COOKIE BOOTH ☐ EVENT:		
M T W TH F SAT SUN	☐ MEETING ☐ COOKIE BOOTH ☐ EVENT:		

"Knowing what needs to be done does away with fear."
— ROSA PARKS

NOTES FOR VOLUNTEERS:

DATE & TIME	MEETING / EVENT	# OF VOLUNTEERS NEEDED	VOLUNTEER NAMES & PHONE NUMBERS
M T W TH F SAT SUN	☐ MEETING ☐ COOKIE BOOTH ☐ EVENT:		
M T W TH F SAT SUN	☐ MEETING ☐ COOKIE BOOTH ☐ EVENT:		
M T W TH F SAT SUN	☐ MEETING ☐ COOKIE BOOTH ☐ EVENT:		
M T W TH F SAT SUN	☐ MEETING ☐ COOKIE BOOTH ☐ EVENT:		
M T W TH F SAT SUN	☐ MEETING ☐ COOKIE BOOTH ☐ EVENT:		
M T W TH F SAT SUN	☐ MEETING ☐ COOKIE BOOTH ☐ EVENT:		
M T W TH F SAT SUN	☐ MEETING ☐ COOKIE BOOTH ☐ EVENT:		
M T W TH F SAT SUN	☐ MEETING ☐ COOKIE BOOTH ☐ EVENT:		

VOLUNTEER SIGN-UP

THANK YOU!

NOTES FOR VOLUNTEERS:

DATE & TIME	MEETING / EVENT	# OF VOLUNTEERS NEEDED	VOLUNTEER NAMES & PHONE NUMBERS
M T W TH F SAT SUN	☐ MEETING ☐ COOKIE BOOTH ☐ EVENT:		
M T W TH F SAT SUN	☐ MEETING ☐ COOKIE BOOTH ☐ EVENT:		
M T W TH F SAT SUN	☐ MEETING ☐ COOKIE BOOTH ☐ EVENT:		
M T W TH F SAT SUN	☐ MEETING ☐ COOKIE BOOTH ☐ EVENT:		
M T W TH F SAT SUN	☐ MEETING ☐ COOKIE BOOTH ☐ EVENT:		
M T W TH F SAT SUN	☐ MEETING ☐ COOKIE BOOTH ☐ EVENT:		
M T W TH F SAT SUN	☐ MEETING ☐ COOKIE BOOTH ☐ EVENT:		
M T W TH F SAT SUN	☐ MEETING ☐ COOKIE BOOTH ☐ EVENT:		

"You can never leave footprints that last if you are always walking on tiptoe."
LEYMAH GBOWEE

NOTES FOR VOLUNTEERS:

DATE & TIME	MEETING / EVENT	# OF VOLUNTEERS NEEDED	VOLUNTEER NAMES & PHONE NUMBERS
M T W TH F SAT SUN	☐ MEETING ☐ COOKIE BOOTH ☐ EVENT:		
M T W TH F SAT SUN	☐ MEETING ☐ COOKIE BOOTH ☐ EVENT:		
M T W TH F SAT SUN	☐ MEETING ☐ COOKIE BOOTH ☐ EVENT:		
M T W TH F SAT SUN	☐ MEETING ☐ COOKIE BOOTH ☐ EVENT:		
M T W TH F SAT SUN	☐ MEETING ☐ COOKIE BOOTH ☐ EVENT:		
M T W TH F SAT SUN	☐ MEETING ☐ COOKIE BOOTH ☐ EVENT:		
M T W TH F SAT SUN	☐ MEETING ☐ COOKIE BOOTH ☐ EVENT:		
M T W TH F SAT SUN	☐ MEETING ☐ COOKIE BOOTH ☐ EVENT:		

VOLUNTEER SIGN-UP

THANK YOU!

NOTES FOR VOLUNTEERS:

DATE & TIME	MEETING / EVENT	# OF VOLUNTEERS NEEDED	VOLUNTEER NAMES & PHONE NUMBERS
M T W TH F SAT SUN	☐ MEETING ☐ COOKIE BOOTH ☐ EVENT:		
M T W TH F SAT SUN	☐ MEETING ☐ COOKIE BOOTH ☐ EVENT:		
M T W TH F SAT SUN	☐ MEETING ☐ COOKIE BOOTH ☐ EVENT:		
M T W TH F SAT SUN	☐ MEETING ☐ COOKIE BOOTH ☐ EVENT:		
M T W TH F SAT SUN	☐ MEETING ☐ COOKIE BOOTH ☐ EVENT:		
M T W TH F SAT SUN	☐ MEETING ☐ COOKIE BOOTH ☐ EVENT:		
M T W TH F SAT SUN	☐ MEETING ☐ COOKIE BOOTH ☐ EVENT:		
M T W TH F SAT SUN	☐ MEETING ☐ COOKIE BOOTH ☐ EVENT:		

"A good compromise is one where everybody makes a contribution."
— ANGELA MERKEL

NOTES FOR VOLUNTEERS:

DATE & TIME	MEETING / EVENT	# OF VOLUNTEERS NEEDED	VOLUNTEER NAMES & PHONE NUMBERS
M T W TH F SAT SUN	☐ MEETING ☐ COOKIE BOOTH ☐ EVENT:		
M T W TH F SAT SUN	☐ MEETING ☐ COOKIE BOOTH ☐ EVENT:		
M T W TH F SAT SUN	☐ MEETING ☐ COOKIE BOOTH ☐ EVENT:		
M T W TH F SAT SUN	☐ MEETING ☐ COOKIE BOOTH ☐ EVENT:		
M T W TH F SAT SUN	☐ MEETING ☐ COOKIE BOOTH ☐ EVENT:		
M T W TH F SAT SUN	☐ MEETING ☐ COOKIE BOOTH ☐ EVENT:		
M T W TH F SAT SUN	☐ MEETING ☐ COOKIE BOOTH ☐ EVENT:		
M T W TH F SAT SUN	☐ MEETING ☐ COOKIE BOOTH ☐ EVENT:		

SNACK SIGN-UP

THANK YOU!

SNACK SUGGESTIONS:

INGREDIENTS TO AVOID:

PLEASE BRING SNACKS FOR .... PEOPLE.

DATE	MEETING / EVENT	VOLUNTEER NAME & PHONE NUMBER
	☐ MEETING ☐ EVENT:	
	☐ MEETING ☐ EVENT:	
	☐ MEETING ☐ EVENT:	
	☐ MEETING ☐ EVENT:	
	☐ MEETING ☐ EVENT:	
	☐ MEETING ☐ EVENT:	
	☐ MEETING ☐ EVENT:	
	☐ MEETING ☐ EVENT:	
	☐ MEETING ☐ EVENT:	
	☐ MEETING ☐ EVENT:	
	☐ MEETING ☐ EVENT:	
	☐ MEETING ☐ EVENT:	
	☐ MEETING ☐ EVENT:	

SNACK SIGN-UP

THANK YOU!

SNACK SUGGESTIONS:

INGREDIENTS TO AVOID:

PLEASE BRING SNACKS FOR .... PEOPLE.

DATE	MEETING / EVENT	VOLUNTEER NAME & PHONE NUMBER
	☐ MEETING ☐ EVENT:	
	☐ MEETING ☐ EVENT:	
	☐ MEETING ☐ EVENT:	
	☐ MEETING ☐ EVENT:	
	☐ MEETING ☐ EVENT:	
	☐ MEETING ☐ EVENT:	
	☐ MEETING ☐ EVENT:	
	☐ MEETING ☐ EVENT:	
	☐ MEETING ☐ EVENT:	
	☐ MEETING ☐ EVENT:	
	☐ MEETING ☐ EVENT:	
	☐ MEETING ☐ EVENT:	
	☐ MEETING ☐ EVENT:	

VOLUNTEER DRIVER LOG

NAME: .... ☐ BACKGROUND CHECK

PHONE: (......)................ **DRIVER'S LICENSE #:** .... **EXPIRATION:** ....../....../...... **LICENSE PLATE:** ....

VEHICLE YEAR, MAKE & MODEL: .... **# OF PASSENGER SEATBELTS:** ....

CAR INSURANCE COMPANY: .... **POLICY #:** .... **EXPIRATION:** ....../....../......

DRIVING LOG:

DATE	EVENT/DESTINATION	DRIVER SIGNATURE	TROOP LEADER SIGNATURE

NAME: .... ☐ BACKGROUND CHECK

PHONE: (......)................ **DRIVER'S LICENSE #:** .... **EXPIRATION:** ....../....../...... **LICENSE PLATE:** ....

VEHICLE YEAR, MAKE & MODEL: .... **# OF PASSENGER SEATBELTS:** ....

CAR INSURANCE COMPANY: .... **POLICY #:** .... **EXPIRATION:** ....../....../......

DRIVING LOG:

DATE	EVENT/DESTINATION	DRIVER SIGNATURE	TROOP LEADER SIGNATURE

"When you're knocked down, get right back up and never listen to anyone who says you shouldn't go on."
— HILLARY CLINTON

NAME: .... ☐ BACKGROUND CHECK

PHONE: (......).................. **DRIVER'S LICENSE #:**.............................. **EXPIRATION:** ....../....../...... **LICENSE PLATE:**..............................

VEHICLE YEAR, MAKE & MODEL:.. **# OF PASSENGER SEATBELTS:**..............

CAR INSURANCE COMPANY:............................ **POLICY #:**............................ **EXPIRATION:** ....../....../......

DRIVING LOG:

DATE	EVENT/DESTINATION	DRIVER SIGNATURE	TROOP LEADER SIGNATURE

NAME: .... ☐ BACKGROUND CHECK

PHONE: (......).................. **DRIVER'S LICENSE #:**.............................. **EXPIRATION:** ....../....../...... **LICENSE PLATE:**..............................

VEHICLE YEAR, MAKE & MODEL:.. **# OF PASSENGER SEATBELTS:**..............

CAR INSURANCE COMPANY:............................ **POLICY #:**............................ **EXPIRATION:** ....../....../......

DRIVING LOG:

DATE	EVENT/DESTINATION	DRIVER SIGNATURE	TROOP LEADER SIGNATURE

VOLUNTEER DRIVER LOG

NAME: .... ☐ BACKGROUND CHECK

PHONE: (......) .... **DRIVER'S LICENSE #:** .... **EXPIRATION:** ...../...../..... **LICENSE PLATE:** ....

VEHICLE YEAR, MAKE & MODEL: .... **# OF PASSENGER SEATBELTS:** ....

CAR INSURANCE COMPANY: .... **POLICY #:** .... **EXPIRATION:** ...../...../.....

DRIVING LOG:

DATE	EVENT/DESTINATION	DRIVER SIGNATURE	TROOP LEADER SIGNATURE

NAME: .... ☐ BACKGROUND CHECK

PHONE: (......) .... **DRIVER'S LICENSE #:** .... **EXPIRATION:** ...../...../..... **LICENSE PLATE:** ....

VEHICLE YEAR, MAKE & MODEL: .... **# OF PASSENGER SEATBELTS:** ....

CAR INSURANCE COMPANY: .... **POLICY #:** .... **EXPIRATION:** ...../...../.....

DRIVING LOG:

DATE	EVENT/DESTINATION	DRIVER SIGNATURE	TROOP LEADER SIGNATURE

"The question isn't who is going to let me; it's who is going to stop me."
— AYN RAND

NAME: .... ☐ BACKGROUND CHECK

PHONE: (......)................... DRIVER'S LICENSE #:........................... EXPIRATION: ...../...../..... LICENSE PLATE: ....

VEHICLE YEAR, MAKE & MODEL:.. # OF PASSENGER SEATBELTS: ....

CAR INSURANCE COMPANY:................................ POLICY #:................................ EXPIRATION: ...../...../.....

DRIVING LOG:

DATE	EVENT/DESTINATION	DRIVER SIGNATURE	TROOP LEADER SIGNATURE

NAME: .... ☐ BACKGROUND CHECK

PHONE: (......)................... DRIVER'S LICENSE #:........................... EXPIRATION: ...../...../..... LICENSE PLATE: ....

VEHICLE YEAR, MAKE & MODEL:.. # OF PASSENGER SEATBELTS: ....

CAR INSURANCE COMPANY:................................ POLICY #:................................ EXPIRATION: ...../...../.....

DRIVING LOG:

DATE	EVENT/DESTINATION	DRIVER SIGNATURE	TROOP LEADER SIGNATURE

VOLUNTEER DRIVER LOG

NAME: .... ☐ BACKGROUND CHECK

PHONE: (......)............... **DRIVER'S LICENSE #:**........................... **EXPIRATION:** ....../....../...... **LICENSE PLATE:**...........................

VEHICLE YEAR, MAKE & MODEL:........................... **# OF PASSENGER SEATBELTS:**...............

CAR INSURANCE COMPANY:........................... **POLICY #:**........................... **EXPIRATION:** ....../....../......

DRIVING LOG:

DATE	EVENT/DESTINATION	DRIVER SIGNATURE	TROOP LEADER SIGNATURE

NAME: .... ☐ BACKGROUND CHECK

PHONE: (......)............... **DRIVER'S LICENSE #:**........................... **EXPIRATION:** ....../....../...... **LICENSE PLATE:**...........................

VEHICLE YEAR, MAKE & MODEL:........................... **# OF PASSENGER SEATBELTS:**...............

CAR INSURANCE COMPANY:........................... **POLICY #:**........................... **EXPIRATION:** ....../....../......

DRIVING LOG:

DATE	EVENT/DESTINATION	DRIVER SIGNATURE	TROOP LEADER SIGNATURE

> *"Change your life today. Don't gamble on the future. Act now without delay."*
> — SIMONE DE BEAUVOIR

NAME: ☐ BACKGROUND CHECK

PHONE: (......) .... **DRIVER'S LICENSE #:** .... **EXPIRATION:** ....../....../...... **LICENSE PLATE:** ....

VEHICLE YEAR, MAKE & MODEL: .... **# OF PASSENGER SEATBELTS:** ....

CAR INSURANCE COMPANY: .... **POLICY #:** .... **EXPIRATION:** ....../....../......

DRIVING LOG:

DATE	EVENT/DESTINATION	DRIVER SIGNATURE	TROOP LEADER SIGNATURE

NAME: ☐ BACKGROUND CHECK

PHONE: (......) .... **DRIVER'S LICENSE #:** .... **EXPIRATION:** ....../....../...... **LICENSE PLATE:** ....

VEHICLE YEAR, MAKE & MODEL: .... **# OF PASSENGER SEATBELTS:** ....

CAR INSURANCE COMPANY: .... **POLICY #:** .... **EXPIRATION:** ....../....../......

DRIVING LOG:

DATE	EVENT/DESTINATION	DRIVER SIGNATURE	TROOP LEADER SIGNATURE

VOLUNTEER DRIVER LOG

NAME: .... ☐ BACKGROUND CHECK

PHONE: (......).................. DRIVER'S LICENSE #:.................................. EXPIRATION: ....../....../...... LICENSE PLATE:..................................

VEHICLE YEAR, MAKE & MODEL:.. # OF PASSENGER SEATBELTS: ....

CAR INSURANCE COMPANY:................................ POLICY #:.. EXPIRATION: ....../....../......

DRIVING LOG:

DATE	EVENT/DESTINATION	DRIVER SIGNATURE	TROOP LEADER SIGNATURE

NAME: .... ☐ BACKGROUND CHECK

PHONE: (......).................. DRIVER'S LICENSE #:.................................. EXPIRATION: ....../....../...... LICENSE PLATE:..................................

VEHICLE YEAR, MAKE & MODEL:.. # OF PASSENGER SEATBELTS: ....

CAR INSURANCE COMPANY:................................ POLICY #:.. EXPIRATION: ....../....../......

DRIVING LOG:

DATE	EVENT/DESTINATION	DRIVER SIGNATURE	TROOP LEADER SIGNATURE

"You have to trust in what you think. If you splinter yourself and try to please everyone, you can't."
ANNIE LEIBOVITZ

NAME: □ BACKGROUND CHECK

PHONE: (......)................. DRIVER'S LICENSE #:........................... EXPIRATION: ...../...../...... LICENSE PLATE:..................

VEHICLE YEAR, MAKE & MODEL:....................................... # OF PASSENGER SEATBELTS:..............

CAR INSURANCE COMPANY:............................... POLICY #:............................... EXPIRATION: ...../...../......

DRIVING LOG:

DATE	EVENT/DESTINATION	DRIVER SIGNATURE	TROOP LEADER SIGNATURE

NAME: □ BACKGROUND CHECK

PHONE: (......)................. DRIVER'S LICENSE #:........................... EXPIRATION: ...../...../...... LICENSE PLATE:..................

VEHICLE YEAR, MAKE & MODEL:....................................... # OF PASSENGER SEATBELTS:..............

CAR INSURANCE COMPANY:............................... POLICY #:............................... EXPIRATION: ...../...../......

DRIVING LOG:

DATE	EVENT/DESTINATION	DRIVER SIGNATURE	TROOP LEADER SIGNATURE

CPSIA information can be obtained
at www.ICGtesting.com
Printed in the USA
LVHW030749091019
633406LV00004B/1382/P